A Comedic ...
a Comedian Until Someone Laughs

Ian Arnison-Phillips

Published by Department of English, Manchester Metropolitan University
www.hlss.mmu.ac.uk/english/acwe
Manchester, 2005

Cover design by Steve Kelly, MMU Design Studio

ISBN: 1-905476-03-5

Jackie

Best Wishes

Ian Arnison-Phillips

For all the family,
especially for Grandad Jim.

"From an early age I've made you smile,
when you felt down you sat with me for a while.
Listened and watched me fool about the place,
my real feelings I hid from my face.
Hidden well behind my smile you see,
as long as people laughed it did not matter to me.
Now my pleasure is from a bottle or no more,
life has presented me with a door.
If I walk through I am no longer fun,
no joke, no gaff, no ending pun,
see,
a comedian aint a comedian till someone laughs my son.

1

Me, My Dad and My Dad's Blue

Manchester. Home of comedians such as the controversial Bernard Manning, loveable Les Dawson and fantastic Peter Kay. Two of them a bit before my time but I've been told they're funny and let's face it, who or what else good has come out of Manchester apart from Liam & Noel Gallagher and Manchester City? When I mean good, I mean something worth shouting about, something you can't replace. Sure, Boddingtons, cream of Manchester, is the best thing to come out of Strangeways but that could be replaced by a jar of Tetleys if that's your poison. Comedians are something you couldn't replace - who else would joke about the 'big light' and family holidays the way Peter Kay does? Comedians have always been people I've admired and so my aim in life was always to be one. John Massey, the funny man.

From the age of about seven I always tried to make people laugh and smile, something that took some work especially since at that age all my friends thought backsides were hilarious. Most of them find backsides hilarious at the age they are now, and I'd still pull a moony in the teacher's face for laughs now or in twenty years time. I never regretted that week's detention. However, I didn't do it again for a while; something told me baring my behind with my dad's punishing belt marks across it wouldn't go down a treat. That was my dad all over; words from the mouth said nothing like his hands did when punishing you. Making people laugh got easier as I got older and became natural to me; this was a statement my old man wished he could make. He was also a comedian, well, a part time pub stand up, but he tried so hard every night to get noticed. This made my desire to get to the top level burn so much more.

I remember walking into my dad's flat one day - he didn't live with us - to find him frantically pulling on a suit because news that Billy Bob had pulled out of a comedy night down at Chubby Racers left a gap in the night's performance.

"Y'alright Dad?" I asked, not expecting a reply.

"Am I alright? Am I alright? I'll let ya know by the end of the night, lad," he replied, rushing about the place trying to find his bow tie. I was about to wish him good luck but I noticed he wasn't there anymore and had left the door ajar. I watched him through the window running down the street, the way dads do, never in a straight line. I turned and observed the flat around me; it was obvious he hadn't had a female's presence in the place for a while. Dirty clothes crowded the floor, unfinished take-away meals spread around the place made it smell anything but wild orchid. However he had made an attempt to make the room smell ok - maybe he'd had company earlier in the week as a vanilla pine tree hung from the lamp shade. It actually looked as if it belonged, as the whole place seemed to be a car crash. This was rummaging time. I thought it was best I stayed away from the bedroom; there was more tissue in there than the bathroom. I avoided that also; I was sure if I entered something would look up at me and call me mama. I stayed in the main room even though there was nothing of real interest in there, apart from his blue films. It's so amusing the way dads try to hide their blue. Normally you would find it on a tape with no box but a white label down the side with a programme name written on it. The programme either doesn't exist or you know no-one ever watches it. My dad had written, 'Last of The Summer Wine,' on his so it wasn't so hard to work out. The old man was out for at least an hour, Kleenex tissues by the couch, why not?

I was woken with a start three hours later by my dad staggering in, bottle in hand and a loose bow tie. I looked up quickly and then breathed a sigh of relief as the video had finished and all that was displayed on the screen were the annoying grey fuzzy lines that make your eyes cross. I looked towards my dad; he didn't look healthy as he stumbled across the room and into his bedroom without a word and collapsed on his bed. He had failed to impress, again. I knew this was my time to leave. He and I did not get on at the best of times never mind when he was completely pissed and depressed about a hard comedy night out. I walked home along Burnage Lane towards my home, kicking stones as I went trying to think of any way at all I could help my dad. I was really worried about him, he was borderline alcoholic, (borderline between George Best and Oliver Reed) smoking 40 a day and extremely depressed. I didn't have time to think a lot because before I knew it my nose was at a level with the number three on the front of my door. I would have to clear my head and put on a smile before I walked into me Mam or she'd moan or ask questions. I didn't tell her where I'd been. I walked in to find my two brothers slouching on the settee watching the telly, not an abnormal sight whatsoever. They spent so much time there motionlessly fixed to the screen, me Mam often checked if they were still breathing. The indentation in the settee where they sat was so big you could fall in it.

"Find a use for yourselves instead of just sitting there or I'll plug you in and use you two as lamps," me Mam used to say. They soon shifted when she shouted round the house that tea was ready; gold winning sprinters could not have sat around the table quicker.

My two brothers named Steven and Peter sat across the table from me. Steven was one year younger than me and Peter, six. Finally we were joined by my 15-year old sister Samantha. I tended to stay away from her. If I was to cook a soup that was delicious, nice with sunshine and daisies I would not have girls, puberty, hormones and periods as part of my recipe. Fear of death kept me away from her. I loved her deep down, though, and behind the lethal stare I could see she loved me too.

I was eighteen at the time and the oldest, apart from me

Mam of course. She eventually joined the table looking her usual rough and over-worked self. She worked hard to keep our nearly crumbling family together and mostly did a great job; everyone in the family respected her for that.

"Where you been John?" she asked as she ate.

"Err, out an' about," I replied hesitantly.

"Out an' about…where?" she asked inquisitively. She knew I was keeping something.

"Well y'know, here and there," I replied once again.

"You've been to his again haven't you!?" she shouted and before I could even begin to lie she got up and took her plate to the living room.

"Why dint you make up a story, knob head?" asked Steven, half laughing.

"I wasn't given a bloody chance. D'you think I have Kelly Holmes runnin' round my mind? She was up and out before she finished her sentence," I protested. I hate that, people who talk to you from another room or as they're walking into one. It's a trick a lot of women pull with their husbands, say something to them when he's half way up the stairs and when he turns around and asks to repeat, they say "You never listen!"

"What was you doin' round his flat anyway?" asked Sam with a stare cold enough to give me arthritis. I didn't reply to this, instead I pushed my food aside and went to sit in the back garden for a while. I knew if I even tried to answer that it would end up in a big argument because none of my family liked my dad. No one ever bothered to see him, ask how he was or send him Christmas presents. I didn't want to grow up never knowing my dad, even if he didn't want to know me. In the corner of my eye I could see two other eyes staring at me while I was thinking; they were the eyes of Peter's rabbit. I turned towards the animal as it just sat there in its cage and looked cute. I don't mean to be a scrooge but come on, what is the point in this pathetic creature? It sits, eats and shits. It rolls around its own muck in its cage all day then its owner picks it up and kisses it. Why can't I sit in my own shit all day, looking cute and get placed on a visiting girl's breasts for a cuddle? Bloody rabbit.

After a while I realised I had been out quite some time thinking of evil, bunny-killing plots and other insane things while it was getting dark. I went back inside and made my way up to my room, the best place in the world to me at that time. It was like a home away from home but in my home, if that makes any sense. This is where you could find all my jokes, puns and work all over the place. On my bed were five pages of material I had frantically been revising ahead of a show I was going to do at the comedy club in town the next day. It was my first show and the thought of it made me scared but excited at the same time. I had no real problem with getting on stage in front of people no matter how big the crowd; it was more the fact I was worried about forgetting my material that made me scared. I have the worst memory in the world, consequently I walk around with trousers two sizes too small, Post-it notes in my pocket and a wife called Jean, Suzie, Janet, Helen and Julie. Bad memory makes you no good with names.

If I forgot anything funny to say on stage I would stutter and have to improvise, which I could do, but for an hour and half I think I'd struggle. I lay on my bed for hours revising and writing new material, "My uncle's fiftieth birthday last week, he got a draft…nah it's already been done." I continued in this manner for ages until I realised it was getting late and lack of sleep would not help my nerves or memory for the day to come. I threw down my pages, climbed in between my sheets and lay there looking at the ceiling for a while. Odd rays of light from the outside street lamp seeped through my half closed blinds; they invaded the dark room but could not conquer it. Thoughts of, "Why does your mum talk posh on the phone to bank people?" echoed around my fading mind as I fell into a slumber.

2

The match and the menopause

The next morning I woke to the smell of nothing - typical - me Mam still in bed and my own bacon to cook. It's amazing how everyone is too tired to make me breakfast on my big day but are sat at the table fresh eyed and smiling when the bacon's ready. It didn't bother me today though; I would let nothing bother me on my big day. The table was in the dining room which was directly opposite the kitchen through an archway.

"You comin' to my show tonight, Mam?" I shouted through the hallway to see if she was talking to me yet.

"I'm so sorry, dear, but your Aunt Jean's round tonight with the gang, you know how it is," she replied, with a sorry look on her face.

"Of course, how could I forget, sitting round a room with a load of ladies who have waistline sizes fit for pensions talking about the menopause - much more important than my comedy night," I said, as Steven laughed with a mouthful of

9

food and Peter looked confused.

"What's a menopause?" Peter quizzed.

"Never mind, eat your breakfast, and as for you, sarcastic swine, we don't sit and talk about the menopause," explained me Mam with a slight smile on her face as she rushed about the place tidying odd things up.

"So you're not denying they're all fat then?" I said. I got no reply. "You comin' to me show then, Ste?"

"Wouldn't miss it for the world mate, should be funny," he said.

"Really?" I asked.

"Yeah, watchin' you die on your arse," he snorted. Peter laughed and spat milk all over the table; I smiled at Steven and put up a sly finger behind my back. Before he could retaliate Peter interrupted, "Can I come to your show, John?"

"Sure, as long as you ask your…" I began.

"No! You're too young," me Mam said before I could continue.

"Wow, did you ask Mam through your mind or something?" I joked. "I'd let you come anytime mate but it's a pub bar kind a thing. They won't let you in and besides it'll be jokes all about the menopause," I said bowling a smile across the room to me Mam who batted one back at me. The whole atmosphere that morning was good, which wasn't portrayed in the slightest by Samantha as the room was graced with her presence.

"You comin' tonight Sam?" I asked. A look of death shot me right in the face. "Err, no then? Well enjoy your night, then," I said. Another shot of death hit me just in case I was still breathing. "Or not…don't enjoy your night, then…oh never mind," I jittered while walking out of the room to avoid the look of 'kick me while I'm down'.

After breakfast I got dressed and thought I had better go and see if my dad was still breathing. So I set off back down Burnage Lane making sure as I left the house no one spotted me to avoid a game of twenty questions. Every time I made the journey it seemed to get shorter, but not that day. Walking past the paper shop I spotted two girls by the bus stop across the other side of the road. Now I don't mean to be arrogant, but being a funny guy has a great advantage with most girls. All the girls I ever pulled were reeled in by my humour…and my good looks, of course. I crossed over the road and headed towards the bus stop. "Excuse me…you must be so embarrassed but I'm sorry, the beautiful bus doesn't pass through here," I quipped with a cheesy smile. What? Yeah, alright, that was awful but I was eighteen, ok? Well anyway, the two girls giggled and turned to each other. Typical. As if the situation of meeting girls isn't hard enough, girls going all quiet and shy doesn't help much either. I just stood there wondering whether the giggles were inviting ones or whether they were just simply laughing at me. It was weird, that despite all the girls I had met, flirted with or gone out with the awkwardness of meeting them for the first time was always there; although it undoubtedly became easier over time. The two girls eventually broke what seemed to be an everlasting silence.

"Oh, does it not?" one of them smirked. "Well that's alrite, we're not catching that bus today."

"Aw, I bet the driver's missin' you."

"Bet he is," the other girl said, still laughing. I still wasn't sure if they were just laughing at me.

"Well what's your names, then?" I asked, switching to a more serious mode. I found out their names were Julia and Chez through a fit of more chuckles. I told them my name and about the comedy gig I was doing.

"You're a comedian?" asked Chez, her interest suddenly sparking.

"Not yet, it's my first gig. Fancy comin?" They turned to one another and had a little quiet discussion. I watched them both as they smiled and glanced at me. I was starting to wonder if this was just a complete waste of time.

"We might do if we have time," said Julia in a teasing tone.

"Sorted." After a while I said my "see you laters" and crossed back over the road and continued my walk. "Oh what a complete tosser you look right now, you thick prat," I said to myself, quietly, as I realized by crossing back over the girls knew I purposely went over to them. "Never mind, keep walking," I sighed.

I walked through the opened door of my dad's flat to find him sat in his dressing gown watching the telly, surrounded by empty cans, bottles and ash trays. He spotted me and murmured in surprise, "What are you doing here?"

"I came to see if you were still alive," I announced.

"Yeah, well I'm talking and passing wind so I guess I'm alive, anything else, doctor?" he snarled sarcastically.

"Well, I'm sorry for showing concern - bloody hell! – anyway, got some news for you."

"Oh, really?" he said without looking at me or showing any real interest.

"Yeah, I'm doing a show down comedy club tonight and I was wondering if…" I began to say before he interrupted, "You're doing what where?"

"I'm…doing…a…show…at the comedy….club," I said rolling my eyes.

"Oh and you thought you'd come rub it in did you?" he proclaimed.

"No, no, that's not what I was doing at all, Dad, I was…" I began once again before he interrupted.

"Don't call me that!" he shouted. "In fact, get the hell out of here now!" he screamed as he pushed me in the gut.

The door behind me swallowed me whole as I fell backwards and a sharp pain echoed around my head as it connected with the doorframe on the way down. The couch cushioned my dad's fall as his unsteady feet also collapsed underneath him. It was clear that his behaviour could not be blamed on the rage of a hangover as he was still wasted, or what had become known as normal. The door was shut in my face and I climbed to my feet, holding my head and made my way back home slowly. I didn't know why, but for some reason I wanted to help this man, despite the hatred I had for him. I mean I loved him deep down, but he never showed any interest in me anymore, never mind love. I wanted that love. More than that, I wanted the weekly pocket money he owed me from the last ten years. However, the help that man needed was beyond my skills, well at that time, anyway.

When I returned home any thoughts of my dad were wiped from my mind by the sight of my best friend Darren sitting on my doorstep rolling a cigarette. He was the same age as me and we'd grown up together. Darren had short black hair, a goatee beard and, as he often told people, was rather good looking.

"What you doin' there, Daz?" I asked.

"Rollin' cig," he murmured quietly whilst the concentration invaded his face.

"Oh really? And here's me thinking you were solving world hunger," I said with sarcasm dripping in my voice.

Darren looked up with a smile and said, "Hey, soz' man, was waiting for ya."

"You can sit inside, you know. What you sat out here for?"

"Sam's in," he replied with a slight cheeky smile.

"Fair play."

"Listen, you know my dad's got two season tickets…well he can't make it to the game this afternoon so I got a spare one if you're interested," he said, knowing exactly what my answer would be. I also knew what the answer would be, but you have to do that pretending to think trick just to make it look like you're an exciting person with a busy schedule. Although I did have a busy night-time schedule, it was three o'clock kick-off so I said, "Meet you outside Wheatsheaf?"

"Sorted…here's your ticket coz' I'll have to dash."

"Alright then, in a bit, mate," I said with a smile from ear to ear.

"Laters," he said and he was off. (For those of you who are not Mancunian, 'In a bit' means goodbye. Tut, southern fairies!) I couldn't believe it, I was as happy as Larry, whoever he is. It was not often I went to see Manchester's finest and I don't mean Trafford United. The Blues are the only team in Manchester and going to see them play was always magical, win or lose. I remember being told before I became a fan that supporting Manchester City was a health risk. I didn't understand at that time but I more than understand now: it's a great unpredictable roller coaster ride. But it was too late - I had signed my life away on the Maine Road contract and now I'm City until I die. Anyway I should press on; I can imagine all the prawn sandwich gobblers (Man United fans) throwing this down in disgust right now. It was one o'clock, practically still morning in my eyes but I would have to rush to meet Darren in the pub by two. You have to get to the pub at least an hour before kick off; it's the law.

If there's anything worse than sitting on a bus in traffic waiting to get to the pub, it's sitting on a bus in traffic waiting to get to the pub with people. There's the mandatory child in a pram at the front crying while the mother talks about Coronation Street last night to her friend. Then there's the old couple at the front who wear tea cozies and obviously think that age is a disability as they take up the disabled person's seats. I don't mean to be awful here but they bounced out of their house, trotted to the bus stop and leapt onto the bus. I'm almost certain they could go those extra steps towards the middle. I chuckled to myself and wrote that down and turned it into a joke. Whilst still smiling I looked out of my window and spotted Samantha.

"Unusual for her to be out in daylight," I murmured to myself. "She must be going to a friend's."

I didn't have the chance to think of any friends she had as the bus stopped at my stop. Vampires only come out at night don't they? I said cheers to the bus driver, stepped off the bus and headed towards the Wheat Sheaf just down the road. I could see Darren sat rolling another cigarette outside.

"Bloody hell," said Darren with a smile.

"What?" I replied confused.

"You've got on a City shirt, City pants, a City jacket and a City hat...you a red then?" he said with a smug smile. "You wanna' drink?" he asked mimicking a drinking motion with his hands and winking at me.

"It's already been done, but yeah, I'll have a drink. This'll be my only one, though. My memory on stage is gonna be bad enough tonight," I said.

"Right, with ya," said Darren with a smile on his face.

"No, I mean it, the last of the last," I said.

Darren looked at me in disgust for a few seconds before turning to the bar shaking his head. I took a seat on one of the outside benches, spinning the beer mats. The picture of a pint glass immediately brought back thoughts of my dad. I had never been to a match with him before, I had always dreamt of it, though. Sitting in the family stand, pie in hand next to the old man, standing up and seeing who could roar blue moon the loudest. Looking back, my first game was with me Mam. How bad is that? I sat there in a raincoat drinking tea from a flask being told by me Mam not to shout.

"There ya go, get that down ya," said Darren upon his return. "You best sup that fast. We should make ar way to stadium soon," he said taking a big gulp from his pint glass. A rim of white froth lay across his top lip.

"Don't say anything, funny man," said Darren knowingly, wiping his mouth with his sleeve.

"I wasn't going to say anything, not really in the funny mood right now."

"You better get that sorted by nine tonight mate," he said, taking another gulp.

"Yeah, I know. It's just my dad, he's worrying me a bit."

"Well, Mr. Massey, we can continue this next week. We're out of time. Come on, we best dash," he said sarcastically. That was typical Darren, never liked talking about problems, rolling fags sorts his problems out. I downed my pint quick and set off towards heaven.

Walking up to the stadium I could hear the people inside singing and clapping, I could smell meat pies and beer and feel the excitement in the air. It was too bad that all I could see was the back of a fat lady's head in front of me waiting to get through the turnstiles. Eventually I was at the front of the queue, I looked back at the line behind me and imagined I was the captain of the team leading them out of the tunnel.

17

Smiling broadly I fumbled through my pockets for my ticket, but the smile dropped off my face faster than Barry White's bollocks during puberty. I had forgotten the ticket. I couldn't believe it; I frantically emptied every one of my pockets onto the floor.

"What the hell are you doing?" asked Darren. I turned to him with a blank look on my face.

"I've left the ticket at home," I said quietly.

"You did what!?" he shouted. I kicked the gloves that fell from my pocket in disgrace. "A shirt, yes, your keys, yes, money, yes, but one thing you don't forget when coming to a match is your bloody ticket, ya fool," he barked.

"Listen, you go in, I'll ring me Mam, tell her to bring ticket and I'll meet you inside, we've still got half hour yet," I said calmly. He sighed, nodded his head and went inside muttering something I couldn't hear. I left the stadium and crossed the road to the nearest phone box and called me Mam. I hoped that her gang was round our house because she couldn't drive. Luckily they were and she sent Jean with the ticket.

I waited outside the stadium for ten minutes and it started to rain, glorious Manchester weather. I was only stood in it for a little while when Jean arrived and passed me the ticket with a disappointed look on her face, "I don't know, where would you be without me, eh?" she said. I smiled and said, "Thanks, Aunty Jean." She wasn't my real Aunty but she was a close family friend so we called her that. I took the ticket, said goodbye and ran towards the stadium and through the turnstiles. It was still 15 minutes before kick-off and Darren was waiting near the bar. He acknowledged I was there and shouted over the crowd, "Hold on here, goin' for a slash."

I looked around at all the people and spotted the opening towards the stands. I peered through and I saw the centre circle and some players I didn't recognize warming up. It was only then I realized I didn't even know who we were playing so I glanced up towards the bookies. It read City to win 6/4 and Newcastle to win 7/4. How any bookies could make any predictions or odds on City was beyond me.

"We got Toon," I said to Darren on his return.

"I know, didn't you smell anything odd when we arrived?" he chuckled as he gestured for me to follow him to the stands. I stepped out and took in the amazing view before me. Parts of the crowd were singing, the rain had stopped and the sun had come out lighting up the droplets of water on the grass magically. I looked towards my left and saw a section of fans taunting the Geordies, towards my right I saw all the children with their families. The players were warming up just below us; we had excellent seats, right on the half way line.

"Oh my God, look, Daz its Helen," I said, pointing in her direction. The crowd must have read my mind because they broke out into a huge cry of Helen, Helen ring your bell. If there ever was a living example of a true fan, it would be moulded in the shape of Helen 'The Bell' Turner. Through rain or shine, through thick and thin the 80+ year old had been to every City match as far back as any other fan could remember; ringing her bell at every game. We sat in our seats watching the stadium fill as kick-off drew close. A man in a brown duffel coat sat beside Darren.

"Y'alright, Ken, mate?" Darren said. He then continued to have a little conversation with the man as I just stared at the pitch in wonderment. "Eh, John, this is Ken. He has season ticket too. Sits next to me every game, turns out he's goin' to that comedy club o' yours tonight," said Darren.

"Oh, hello mate," I said and I shook his hands. Just then a voice echoed around the stadium saying, "Ladies and Gentlemen. Please welcome your two teams this afternoon, Manchester City and Newcastle United." The place erupted with a mighty roar as the two teams came out. Game on.

The game was end-to-end football, exciting for the crowd but frustrating for managers. Every now and then a man from the crowd would jump to his seat and shout, "Come on City!!" As if that was any real advice to your team. Could you imagine the manager at half time huddling up and shouting that? It always made me laugh how everyone in the crowd was a referee or a World Cup winning know-it-all. "Why didn't you shoot!?" came another cry from below me. He obviously thought their players were ghosts and the ball would pass right through them. But it was Newcastle so he may have had a point. The game was great, the atmosphere was fantastic but typically we got beat. Walking back towards the pub with a two-one defeat over your head isn't a great way to start a comedy night.

"Your fault," said Darren.

"How is it my fault?" I gasped, "Oh, I'm sorry, you're

right, I should have scored that header," I exclaimed, raising one eyebrow.

"No, but you should have remembered your ticket - you jinxed it," he said, walking into the pub.

"Oh I see," I said laughing, "forgive me."

"If you have another drink I might consider it."

"Nah, I better not, I should be getting back now anyway. I got some revising to do."

"Revising? You're doing stand up comedy, not a bloody maths test," he joked while rolling another cigarette. I looked at him with a disappointed look on my face.

"Alright, alright I'll see you later," he sighed.

"Yeah see ya later, mate," I said returning his season ticket and walking ahead as he went inside the pub. Just before he stepped in I turned around and said, "Oh by the way."

"What?" he snorted with his fag hanging from his lips.

"Those are bad for ya."

"Piss off," he snarled.

I made my way home the same way I came on the bus; once again there was the crying child and the old tea cozy couple. I was beginning to wonder if they came included with the bus, maybe they just never got off. The bus drove past my dad's flat. I tried to look through his window but the lights were off so nothing was clear. I eventually faced my front door just before six o'clock. I could hear me Mam and her gang laughing in the front room as I entered. These were not good revising conditions as laughter and odd vibrating sounds interrupted me; I was curious as to what sort of meeting me Mam had with her gang. I daren't ever ask or look as the possibility of me walking in to see me Mam giggling over a pink '12 incher' knocked me sick. I climbed the stairs towards my room to find Peter playing on the landing with his toy cars.

"Y'alright 'r kid?" I asked.

"Yeah, I heard about City, bad loss," he said, trying to impress.

"Yeah, it was. Tell me, is Sam in?" I enquired.

"No, she went out ages ago."

"She say where?"

"No, I wouldn't want to know either, would you?" he laughed.

I smiled, shook my head and entered my room to find four full bin bags on a put up bed. "What the…" I gasped.

"Don't you swear!" said Peter sternly.

"I wasn't going to!" I shouted, "Mam!"

"Yeah!?" hollered me Mam from downstairs.

"Whose are these bags and this put-up bed in my room!?" I yelled back.

"Oh, they're your uncle Jim's, he's staying for a few nights. Your aunty Jane's threw him out. You mind, love?" she said. My uncle Jim is one of those uncles you only see once a year, which is usually at Christmas when he gives you a radio clock, but he claims that he's the best uncle you've got. On top of all that he was a complete prat. He was forty-nine, thick as loaves and thought he was with it.

"Of course I bloody mind, the man's a fool, tell him he

can't stay because we've got family round that actually see us more than once in a blue bloody moon," I cursed.

"Well, I've kind of already told him he could stay," she replied quietly.

"Oh so you ask if it's alright after you've told him he could stay. Well, that's great, Mam. Tell you what - give us a nice burial when I die of poisoning the in middle of night, he passes gas like an exhaust pipe!" I raged before storming into my room. It was a good job he wasn't there at the time, he was worse when he was in a huff. It wasn't a good start to my night at all and I only had two hours before show time.

24

3

Show Time

I peered into the mirror looking at the man staring back at me in his posh suit, the suit you only wear for weddings and such. There was a knock on my bedroom door and a voice from behind it said, "Guess who's here!?" I sighed. "That's right, it's your favourite uncle!" he shouted as he jumped into the room. I looked at him and sighed again. He was wearing a baseball cap backwards, a leather jacket, a gold chain and faded blue jeans. It was like seeing Elvis Presley and Vanilla Ice mixed into one.

"My, my, don't you shoot up?" he said.

"Oh no, that stain on the curtain's not what you think," I joked.

"What?" said Jim confused.

"Never mind."

"So it looks like me and you are going to be room mates, eh?" he said with a smile.

"Yeah, and as a room it has rules, mostly situated around you," I said sternly.

"How'd you mean?"

"If you touch any of my stuff I'll throw you out, if you bring in anythin' alive I'll throw you out, if you perform any bodily functions in here apart from sleepin' I'll throw you out," I explained. "In fact you're gonna have to try very hard not to get thrown out." Uncle Jim just nodded his head and winked at everything I said. He raised two thumbs and said, "You're the boss."

"Glad we got that sorted. Right, I better get goin', don't want to be late," I said.

"Oh yeah, hurry up. I'll follow you."

"What you mean you'll follow me? I can find my way perfectly, cheers,"

"Yeah but seein' as I'm comin' to see you, I might as well walk with you."

"Oh God," I sighed. With him in the audience there was at least two pages of material about him I couldn't do. I thought it was best not to convince him not to go as I was in a rush so I straightened myself up, picked up my small bag and said, "Lead the way, cowboy."

The journey was very long with my uncle Jim for company; his mouth was motorized. I breathed a huge sigh of relief once I'd got rid of him at the back entrance of the club. He went around the corner to the front entrance as I gathered my thoughts before opening the doors. I walked in to be greeted by the manager, Mr. Stringfellow. (Don't tell me - I know - his poor wife.)

"Ah, John, you're here, your dressing room is just to the

left down there," he said as he pointed down a corridor. I thanked him and made my way towards my dressing room, which was more like a cabinet. It was so small you could join the mile high club in bigger spaces. I didn't have anything to dress into so I used it as a 'check up on your jokes' room instead. I waited nervously. There was only a crowd of around a hundred out there but I was shaking. This could make or break me; many new upcoming great comedians had sprouted from this place. It had the biggest comedy influence in Manchester. The show was going to start with the veteran, Billy Bob. He was known to many in my area, mainly the locals at the pubs. Billy was offered a shot at the big time but he never took it, he was too much of a local man. From my room I could hear him working the audience like puppets; they roared with laughter. Everyone knew if he took the big time he would turn heads. I wish everyone knew that about me.

My turn eventually came and my name was called down the corridor. I got up and shuffled towards the stage. I stood backstage whilst Mr. Stringfellow announced on the microphone my name and such. Finally I was allowed to go on; I shuffled forward and walked up to the mike, looking out at the crowd. I could see Darren sat next to Steven and uncle Jim had a front row seat which worried me a bit. In the middle I spotted a man that I recognized but couldn't put a name to; I was sure I had seen him earlier that day. I was about to pick up the microphone and start to die on my arse when my eyes locked with a blushing girl's eyes. It was that bird from the bus stop; she was with her mate again and both were sending sweet smiles in my direction. I had to get on with it so I cleared my mind and picked up the microphone. Two salty streams of sweat raced against each other down either side of my face. I rubbed my forehead and cheeks shakily with my sleeve. A big damp and dark patch stood out on the arm of my suit. "Sorry for being so wet, but I was told I had a dry sense of humour," I improvised.

The crowd laughed a little. That was just a tester, seeing their level of humour. They laughed a little at that and that was a bad joke, I knew then that they were going to roar at my other material. A sudden burst of confidence sprung from inside me, releasing the butterflies in my stomach. Michael Schumacher must have stepped into the driving seat of my brain as it clicked into the right gear. I began to strut around the stage letting loose all my work, the crowd laughing and cheering. The spotlight directed at me made the crowd a little hard to see as they sat in the dark, but I could make out little pockets of them. At one point, I noticed one of the girls from the bus stop had to be escorted out of the room because she was choking on her drink. This reminded me of the joke about forgetting people's names; the crowd roared once I had told it. I was on stage for about an hour and I didn't stutter once and to see Darren and Steven in tears made it that extra bit special. I couldn't have asked for a better reception. I finished with a, "Goodnight, God bless," and left the stage with a huge smile on my face.

"Ok, if you would like to just sit over there, or you can go through to the front if you want to watch the next act," said a scrawny man backstage. I obliged and went through to the front to sit with Darren and Steve. "That was classic, man!" said Steven rubbing his sides.

"You never told me you were that good," said Darren, smiling.

"Cheers," I replied bashfully. We sat and had a few drinks chatting while the last act got a few laughs here and there, mostly from my idiotic uncle. It wasn't long before the last act deserted the stage, people started to leave and the curtains came down on the stage. I didn't know what to do; I wanted to find out if I was good or if they wanted me back another night. All my life I had wanted to be a comedian; I had built all my dreams up for this one hopeful night and yet I was sat there not knowing if it was a waste of time or not. I sat there with Steven and Darren for a few more minutes as the last of the people left the bar. We were all silent as I twiddled my thumbs and shuffled my feet. Darren and Steven stared at each other lost for words or action. My eyes twitched from door to door, waiting for someone to walk through them.

I turned to Darren, "So what now?" I said.

"Well usually I go home and pleasure myself over the Discovery Channel. What do you mean, what now?" he replied sarcastically.

"I want to know if I was good enough," I protested.

"I already told you, you were great," said Steven.

"No, I mean if I got noticed, if they want me back or not," I replied, getting up out of my seat.

"Where you goin'," Darren and Steven said at the

29

same time.

"To find Mr. Stringfellow," I replied.

I walked through a door beside the stage into the back area with them following me. Mr. Stringfellow was discussing something with another act that had been on that night so I waited for him to finish. I left Steven and Darren to wait by the door.

"You after something?" he asked, once he had finished.

"Oh, yeah I was wondering…if you erm…ya know…thought I was any good tonight?" I asked innocently.

"Well, you certainly made the crowd laugh, son," he replied giving me a playful punch in the arm.

"Well, I was just thinking … I might be a little cheeky asking this on my first show but…" I started, before being interrupted.

"You want to know if you've been recognized. You want to know if we want you back," he said.

I smiled hesitantly and nodded. He put his arm around my shoulder and said, "I'm sorry son, we're just not talent spotting at the moment. You were good, I have to admit, but we already have some talent to be getting on with at this moment in time." He turned me around, "You came two years too late, mate," he said, smiling like a grandad.

I tried taking all his words in but my heart had sunk and my mind had left me. I felt terrible. I said goodbye to Mr. Stringfellow and made my way towards the boys. "Well, what did he say?" asked Steven enthusiastically.

"He said he's not talent spotting," I replied with my head

down. I continued to walk past them and out the front door into the street where it was, predictably, raining. "Wait up!" shouted the boys but I continued to walk, kicking stones along the road as I went. "Listen mate, cheer up, you will get spotted eventually. Tell you what, I'll see you tomorrow. I best run, it's lashing it down," said Darren.

"You won't see me tomorrow. I'm staying in," I replied miserably.

"Oh yes, I will," said Darren with a sly smile on his face and he ran off in the other direction.

I didn't do or say much for the rest of that night. I went straight to bed after I had got home, ignoring my family. I was woken up the next morning by the sound of snoring. I lifted my head slowly to look at the time and it was almost eleven. I turned over to the beautiful sight of uncle Jim sprawled across the put-up bed half naked, in an awkward position fit for the *Kama Sutra*. I picked up a copy of the *Beano* from under my bed and chucked it at his head, hitting him in the face. He snorted loudly, turned around and began dreaming again. I thought I could do the same but just as the room around me faded into darkness behind my tired eyelids there was a bang on the door. "You're jokin," I mumbled to myself, thinking it was the postman. It must have been a package I had to sign for so I clambered out of bed and put my dressing gown on, mumbling as I went down the stairs, "Oh well, better make the most of it, probably the only autograph I'll ever give out." I opened the door and to my surprise there stood Darren and a man I was sure I recognized standing beside him.

"Rise and shine, darlin'. I got someone here to see you," said Darren.

"What you mean, you have someone here to see me?" I quizzed.

"Remember Ken from City match?" replied Darren, gesturing towards the familiar man. I looked at him and said, "Oh yeah, I thought I recognized you mate. What you want to see me for?"

Before Ken could even open his lips, Darren butted in, "He was at your comedy show last night, you see him?" he asked. I thought back and remembered I had seen him in the middle of the crowd; it must have been because he didn't have a duffel coat on. I looked him up and down. He looked much smarter than the times I had seen him before. He had a straight black suit on with a grey shirt and tie. There was an awkward silence. "And...?" I said inquisitively.

"And he liked your..." Darren started to say before being shut up.

"And I liked your show, very much. I think you have a lot of talent, my friend," he said in a gruff voice.

"Well, thank you. I wish other people thought the same," I replied blankly.

"Listen, I'll get right to the point because I'll have to run soon. I'm a busy man," he said. I rolled my eyes. "My name is Ken Rochdale, I own a comedy club called LaughSomeMore in the town centre. I'd like you to come do a show there in front of a few talent spotters and a crowd of around one hundred two nights from now, what you think?" he asked with a little smile. My jaw dropped so low it said hello to my knees.

"Of course…thank you so much Mr. Rochdale," I blurted out while shaking his hands. We stood at my doorstep discussing and arranging some things, my excited mind not really paying attention, before Ken and Darren eventually left. I danced around the hallway as the door shut and bounced up the stairs, waking everyone in the house. I was too awake and happy to go back to bed so I ran back down the stairs into the kitchen to make breakfast.

I reached down to the pan cupboard when I heard a door being shut closed. I peeped through the kitchen door in puzzlement to find Sam walking up the stairs. "Surely she couldn't have gone out before I got up? I would have heard her," I whispered to myself. I thought back to the night before and realized I had not seen her in the house at all before everyone went to bed. At the time I was too depressed to ask questions. The word depressed automatically made my dad pop into my head. I wondered if it was a good idea to go and see him later or not. He probably would have known by that time if I had been spotted because he was always snooping around the Comedy Club. He was desperate to get on stage…or at least to get another pint. I pondered on the idea of telling him I had been spotted by Ken. "Hurry up, Johnny boy!" shouted Steven from the table. I had not even realized he was there, nor Peter whilst I was lost in thought. While eating breakfast I came to the decision that I was going to see my dad - I was curious as to what his reaction would be to my

33

news. I was hoping he'd be happy for me; I wanted to make him proud. But, then again, I had got recognition in one show and he had been trying to get that all of his life. That wasn't something that was going to be easy to take for my dad. However, it was better to tell him than keep it from him, he'd only have a go at me for doing that. I would have to tell him - I wanted to tell him.

4

Dad, Darren and Dibble

I walked with a brisk step on the way to my dad's that day. Excitement had built in me from the news I had got that morning and I couldn't suppress it. I had reached the bus stop when I noticed my trainer laces were untied so I kneeled down to tie them again. Just as I did this a voice from behind me said with a giggle, "You must be so embarrassed but the beautiful bus doesn't pass through here." I turned around to find the girl I had met in the exact same spot yesterday. I looked her up and down briefly, my eyes following all of her curves. She had on a low cut top, tight jeans and was carrying a pink handbag. She smiled and went red.

"Hello gorgeous," I said with surprise, "I saw you in the crowd at the show last night."

"Yeah, I had a great night, you were really good," she said, laughing.

"I try my best." The mandatory awkward silence followed. "I saw your mate choking on her drink."

"I know, she's a daft sod," she snorted. "Mind you, it was your fault, you could have killed her."

"How's that then?"

"You made her laugh."

"Oh well I'm sorry, I'll try be less funny next time," I chuckled. "Hey listen, I'm doin' another show a few nights from now if you fancy comin'. It's not at the same place but maybe afterwards we could go for somethin' to eat or drink somewhere if, you're up for it?" I choked. My balls tightened and practically disappeared into my crotch, watching her eyes roll as she pondered on the date. It was happening again, the anxiety and shyness pulsing through my veins as I asked the question. It's not as if I've never talked to the girl before either, so why was I so nervous? The teenage body is a very confusing and dangerous object; every teenager should have a label saying 'may cause mental torment.'

"Sounds good to me," she said smiling and playfully poking me in the arm. The anxiety flushed from my body and a smile sprung across my face.

"Sorted! Listen, I'll have to get going. I've got to be somewhere. Can I give you my mobile number and I'll tell you where it is?" I asked. She nodded her head and happened to have a receipt I could scribble my number on in her handbag. When I say happened to have a receipt she actually happened to have about a full shop's worth in there.

Honestly, why do women keep so many receipts? I have been shopping with women before - mainly my mother - and from my experience they do enough testing of the product inside the store to know it won't damage when it gets home. For example, when me Mam went shopping for a blouse, she wouldn't pay for one until she had stretched it, wore it, rubbed it, spilt gravy on it, washed and ironed it and practically tested if it was bomb proof. I said goodbye to her and went to walk down the road when I stopped and suddenly realized I had forgotten her name. Could you ask for a better start to an upcoming date? Turning up not even knowing her name, once again my Skoda car memory had failed its MOT. I turned round and said, "Sorry, what's your name again?"

"Oh give over, funny man," she said giggling and she crossed the road waving goodbye. That's the downside to being a comedian - everyone thinks you're always joking. I turned back around and carried on walking trying to remember her name desperately but had no luck as my dad's flat appeared down the road.

I arrived at the door surprised to find that it was shut. I knocked but no reply came. Worried thoughts ran through my head. He could be lying in his own blood or something. I stepped back a few steps, took a run up and kicked the door with all my power. "Ow! You bastard!" I shouted. The door didn't even dent. I didn't fancy another go either so I gave up; I could have sworn the door had a chuffed grin across its panel. I stumbled home with a very unattractive limp, I was glad the girl at the bus stop wasn't around. I got about half way and had to stop. Pain was shooting down the side of my leg; it was a waste of money but I was going to have to get the bus back home. The bus didn't take long and I took the opportunity to take the disabled seats, much to the disapproval of an old couple boarding the bus. The bus set off and I leant my head against the window looking out when I saw Samantha once again. She was sat on a bench outside of a park next to a rather tall looking man in a biker's jacket. He had a messy goatee beard and long tangled hair. They seemed to be talking; I thought they must have been arguing over something as Samantha could start a row with a cardboard box. This could have been true, if she had not leaned over and kissed him.

I bolted upright and pressed my head against the window pane. They were definitely kissing. My stomach flipped. He looked old enough to be her dad. Before I could see anything else or try and do anything the bus moved forward. I sat rigid for the rest of the short journey feeling sick, angry and murderous at the same time. When the bus stopped around the corner of my house I hopped to my door hoping me Mam had a bandage or something to support my leg. I stumbled in and slammed the door shut to find two coppers stood in the living room.

"Oh God, what now?" I blurted whilst I opened the door again, puzzled, and saw the police car outside of the drive; I wondered how I had not seen it on the way in. I shut the door once more and sighed. "What's happening here, Mam?" I asked, as she sat on the settee, flicking a fag and looking unmoved.

"Your dad's been playin' silly buggers again," she replied with a disgusted look.

One of the coppers took out a notebook and said, "We've come here because your dad is in the station along with a Darren Flower Haze who I believe is a companion of yours." I shook my head and sighed again. "Yes he is, why? What has he done?" I asked.

"He has been involved in a fight with your father and is slightly concussed. He has had medical attention but we cannot let him leave the station alone," he explained.

"You're joking, why come to me?" I asked, puzzled.

"We couldn't get in touch with his parents and he asked for you," he replied.

"Right then. I best go then eh?" I sighed, "See you in a bit, Mam." I left the house with the two coppers and I got in the back of the car.

"Let's just hope this is the first and last time you see the back of a police car, son," said the copper who was quiet in the house. They both chuckled.

The journey was short and silent. Before long I was walking through the doors of the station to find Darren sat on some chairs to the right with a bandage on his head.

"What the bloody hell you been playin' at?" I said fiercely.

"Me? What have I been playin at!?" he said innocently.

"Yes you, look at ya, daft prat," I said, sitting beside him.

"I've done nothing, it's your psycho father that's caused all this," he protested. My shoulders dropped.

"Why, what's he done now?" I moaned.

"I saw him in the Wheatsheaf and I told him about you bein' recognized, by Ken, like," he began. "Next minute he's picked up a bar stool and launched it right at me noggin," he screamed.

"Oi, keep it down!" shouted the receptionist.

"Oh God, where is he now?" I asked looking around the place.

"Through that door getting an earful, a warning or something, I don't know. It's my turn next anyway," he said, nursing his head wound and pointing towards a double door. Just as he had said that a woman appeared from behind them and motioned us to come through. We walked towards her and through the doors where I saw my dad with two coppers. The woman told us to sit in a little waiting room on our own. We sat there for a few minutes, silent, whilst he rubbed his head. I started chuckling to myself.

"And just what do you think is funny right now, man?" snorted Darren.

"Your middle name is Flower," I sniggered cheekily.

"Shut up!" he growled. Shortly after he began chuckling too, before being called in to the two coppers.

Darren's presence was replaced by my dad's as he was told to sit in the room. I looked at him for a while as he sat there with his eyes closed. He looked rough, had a scratch across his face and smelt of booze.

"Why did you hit him, Dad?" I asked. There was no reply, instead he just opened his eyes and glared at me. After some time he said, "I heard you got noticed by Mr. Rochdale himself, smug about that, are ya?"

"Well yeah, I'm pretty happy about it," I replied shuffling

my feet. He just shook his head and closed his eyes again. Shortly after Darren came back into the room with the two coppers by his side. "Right, Mr. Massey if you would like to follow me and we will sort out your court time," one of them said before leading him out of the door.

"What does he mean, court time?" I asked puzzled.

"Someone's pressing charges against him," explained Darren.

"Who!?"

"I dunno, someone he hit."

"He hit you!"

"Yeah I know, but apparently I'm not the only one he hit." The remaining copper came closer to us. "Your dad was involved in a number of incidents, with a number of people. One of them is pressing charges against him." I tilted my head back and sighed deeply. There was a short pause before the copper spoke again. "I think it's best you took Darren home or somewhere where you'll be with him, just to be safe," he said. I nodded and we were led out of the station back outside again.

"So where you want to go?" I asked Darren with my hands in my pockets.

"Wheatsheaf," he replied.

42

5

Fireworks at the Fireplace

I woke up on a settee in Darren's living room. I had no idea how I'd got there. I sat up and the headache I received from doing so told me why I didn't know how I'd got there. I held my head and went in search of some aspirin. Walking to the kitchen seemed like walking to my dad's house; Darren's place was really big. My family lived in a three bedroom council house with me Mam sleeping in the spare room downstairs. The house Darren lived in was a private home, a bit posh for Manchester. I eventually found the kitchen and spied some tablets which I gulped down with no water. I was shortly joined by Darren who was still sporting his head bandage and wearing a black dressing gown.

"You look like a nun," I laughed. Darren look startled and surprised to see me.

"I don't remember you coming back here last night," he said, looking confused.

"Let's blame that on the concussion, eh?" I said winking.

He smiled and took the aspirin tablets from my hand.

While Darren was upstairs getting dressed I took a look around some of the rooms in his house. In the living room all the shelves were lined with framed photos of his family. I picked some of them up taking closer looks when Darren returned. "How come your folks aren't in?" I asked.

"They hardly ever are," he replied. "My dad travels the country on his business trips and me Mum has a twelve hour job," he said unmoved. He didn't seem to mind that his parents were never around, he got on by himself. It's just a shame his folks weren't around to see Darren's proudest moments as he was growing up, like having his head splattered with a bar stool and concussing himself.

"Don't you ever wish you had the house to yourself?" he asked, "I know I would if I had your family." I laughed and punched him in the arm playfully.

"What you mean by that then?"

"Well you aint exactly the royals, are ya?" he replied, "and I wouldn't think it was heaven living with that she-devil." I knew that he meant Samantha. I had been friends with Darren since school and he was often tortured by my little sister when he came round to stay. Sam's pet snake resting against your crown jewels at three o'clock in the morning is a little shocking to wake up to and not enjoyable to say the least, unless you're that way inclined, of course. Suddenly the thought of Samantha made me remember what I had seen the day before, "Oh sugar! Listen - I have to get off - speak to you later," I said. I ran into the hall, threw my trainers on and headed out the door before he could reply.

When I arrived home Steven was the first person I came across inside the hallway. "Is Sam in?" I asked hurriedly.

"Yeah. Lucky you caught her, she's gettin' ready to go out," he replied.

"Oh, I have caught her alright, but just to make sure I'm gonna follow her," I said sneakily.

"What you mean, you're gonna follow her?" he asked looking puzzled as I hid under the stairs directly opposite the front door. "Are you feeling ok?" Steven asked, still puzzled.

"Just do one, will ya? I'll tell you in a minute," I whispered fiercely. He stood looking confused as I hid under the stairs shutting the door behind me, then sighed and walked into the living room. I waited inside, breathing softly, looking absolutely mental. The space was only small and packed with my dad's tool boxes from when he used to live with us. He probably forgot to take them with him when he moved out because everyone probably forgot they were there as they were never used. I do not know a dad who actually uses the tools he buys. There were stacks of pliers, screw-drivers, electrical tools, drills and sanders all bought for the main reason of 'you never know.' (If you have ever sat in B&Q and watched all the blokes go by you would notice them pointing at things and saying 'you never know.' Wouldn't it be great if that principle worked in places other than hardware stores? On my list of things to do before I die, I want to walk into a brothel and say 'you never know.' It works on two levels also as you almost definitely don't know what you're getting from a brothel.)

I balanced on one leg, my face pressed up against a tool box and my arm resting on a hose pipe. Suddenly there were thumps on the roof above me sending dust into my eyes; she was coming down the stairs. I slightly opened the door to my secret den and watched her leave through the front door without a word to anyone. I came out from under the stairs and waited in the hall for a few seconds and then went through the door myself. Sam had walked down the road and took a left, towards the park where I spotted her on the bus. I followed her for some time. She walked at a steady pace and I kept a good distance away from her to avoid the risk of being caught. The 'exciting' pursuit ended at the park where she sat at the same bench as the day before. I panned out the area looking for somewhere to hide myself with a good view. I felt like a child again; it was just like playing army with water pistols during the summer. I ducked and moved forward quickly towards a big tree within the park, proper Rambo style. All I needed now was falling rockets, a German, a dead sergeant and Forrest Gump hauling a black bald man over his shoulders. I peered around the tree to find that Sam had been joined by the biker. There was a bench behind theirs, where I could sit with my back to them and listen but not be seen, so I ran towards it stealthily. Once there I raised the collar of my shirt and slouched on the bench straining to hear what they were saying. "Y'alright babes?" I heard Samantha say.

"Babes?" I whispered through gritted teeth. This was language I did not expect from Miss Grim Reaper.

"Yeah I'm sound," the biker replied.

"Sound?" I whispered to myself, searching his accent.

"You been up to much, like?" the biker asked my sister.

"Bloody hell, he's Scouse," I said a little too loudly. Not only that, he looked twice her age.

He turned around quickly and looked behind him. I didn't move a muscle, I didn't even breathe. I couldn't get caught now, not after I had done so well. Luckily he shrugged his shoulders and turned back around. They had a little conversation and I listened until the chat came to a close. I turned to see their lips locked once again. My blood boiled and my face began to burn. I jolted as if electrical currents had been passed through my body, reached behind me over the two benches and pushed his face, crashing him to the ground. "Stop eating my sister's face!" I shouted before jumping over the two benches. He stood up at eye-level with me and shook himself down. "Who the fuckin' hell are you!?" he screamed.

"Well, when I say my sister that kind of makes me her brother doesn't it?" I said sarcastically.

By this time Samantha had shot up and was trying to push me out of the way. No matter how scared of her I was before, I was too angry to think she was any more than just a small girl so I stood my ground. The biker looked at me still puzzled and was about to say something before I interrupted him, "How old are you?" I asked shooting an angry glare his way.

"Twenty-four. What's it got to do with you?"

"Twenty-bleedin'-four!" I shouted. "Do you know how old she is?" I pointed towards Sam who had given up pushing

47

me away and was instead beginning to cry.

"Don't do this, John, please!" she shouted.

I ignored her and asked the biker the same question. "She's eighteen. I thought you would have known that, being her brother like!" he replied sarcastically. I turned towards Samantha; she had her head down kicking the grass beneath her feet with tears rolling down her cheeks.

"Well, what's the problem?" he asked innocently.

"Try knocking three years off that," I said quietly still looking at my sister.

The biker's jaw dropped and he turned towards Samantha, "You told me you were eighteen," he said to her. Samantha said nothing. "Listen mate, I really didn't know. She lied to me all this time," he said protesting his innocence.

I nodded my head, "Sam, start walking home now. I'll catch you up," I said, "and as for you, I don't want to see your face again, you hear me?" I nodded at the biker. Samantha turned around and began walking home as the biker agreed to everything I said. "Oh and one more thing," I said to him.

"What?" he asked. I stepped up to him, pulled my hand back and threw it forward landing it on the bridge of his nose. He went flying back and smashed his head on the bench, blood started to gush down his chin. "Scouse bastard," I said and left the park.

I walked briskly back home with a little satisfactory smile on my face. I spotted Sam drifting home slowly, wiping her face with the sleeve of her jumper so I ran to catch her up. "You know I had to do that," I said to her softly once arriving

48

at her level.

"No you didn't!" she screamed, still sobbing.

"He is twenty-four!" I shouted back at her.

"You should have minded your own business, and you can't stop me from seeing him!" she said whilst running ahead. I knew that what she was saying was true, I couldn't follow her everyday and she wasn't going to listen to me. However I did know someone who could make her listen. Someone with more fire from the deep depths of hell from whence she came. Someone with a bigger attitude than Sam. Someone with bigger claws than Sam. Someone with more buckles in her strait jacket than Sam. This someone was me Mam. Mums are generally not the ladies to mess with, they've been through labour and during the process they've strangely grown an invisible set of cast iron testicles that means they can take on the world. That is the reason why I think the Women's Institute should be banned - a collection of so many mothers could lead to world domination. I walked into my front door to find the very woman stood in the hallway with an accusing look on her face. "What she crying for?" she growled.

"Eh, you can take that look off your face for a start. This has nowt to do with me," I shot back. "She ran upstairs?"

"Yeah, five minutes before you came in," she replied.

"Well, come in here and I'll tell you all about it," I said, gesturing towards the living room door.

I sat me Mam down and proceeded to tell her what I had seen and the events that had gone on that day. Her face looked mortified as she took in every detail without a word or flinch. After I had finished telling I immediately regretted it for I knew exactly what was in store for my sister. My mother got out of her seat and ran upstairs like a bullet. A few seconds later she came storming back down them with Samantha's neck in her hand. I was starting to think I could use them both as a ventriloquist act at my next show. This was no comedy situation though. Me Mam made her stand up against the fireplace and she went to town on her. Of course all the commotion, which could be heard three houses down the road courtesy of me Mam's mouth, caused Steven and Peter to come rushing in. "What's going on?" asked Steven excitedly.

"Shut up you!" me Mam said, without even looking at him. She continued to bomb my sister with insults and questions while she stood there crying and taking it all. "He's old enough to be your father!" she shouted across the room, throwing her slipper towards Sam.

"Who's old enough to be 'er dad?" whispered Peter in my ear.

"Never mind kid," I replied.

"Did I hear someone's a dad?" asked uncle Jim as he walked in the room.

"Oh you're all we need right now," I sighed. He walked across the room and took a seat on the settee. "What would you do if he wanted more than just a peck on the cheek, Sam?" she asked inquisitively, "You know what men are like - it's all they want!"

"Oh God, here we go, I knew she'd say something like that," I sighed quietly to Steven as she continued to hurl abuse at my sister. Steven started laughing; by this time he had clocked on as to what was going on.

"Oh, you mean this grandpa boyfriend she's got?" asked Steven, mocking Sam. His smile soon dropped off his face.

"You mean to say you knew about this?" me Mam asked as her head spun round to shoot a deadly look his way. Just at that unfortunate moment Darren walked through the front door and into the living room. "Oh dear," he murmured as he surveyed the scene. Everyone acknowledged his presence but ignored him. "Well, yeah I did know, Mam," replied Steven worriedly.

"Bloody hell, Ste," I said.

"Then why didn't you say anything!?" yelled me Mam.

"Because she said she'd never let me live it down!" whined Steven with his finger pointing in Sam's direction.

"I'm never going to let you pissin' live it down either, moron!" shouted me Mam. The whole place was turning into a bit of a circus. I told Peter to go out of the room before he got dished some abuse, so he went and sat in the kitchen. There was an awkward silence as everyone stood there.

"Bit of a wrong time then?" said Darren half smiling.

"Shut up Darren!" everyone shouted at the same time, including uncle Jim.

It was late at night before everyone had settled down a bit. Samantha started to realize by the end of me Mam's three hour lecture that what she was doing was wrong. She ended up kissing and making up with me Mam at the end of all the drama. I phoned Darren to apologize. He had left the house and gone home without us realizing until after the fight. After all the peace was made I was ready to go to bed, so I dragged my tired body up the stairs. I opened my bedroom door to the ever so pleasing sight of my uncle Jim lying half naked on his bed. "Haven't you moved out yet?" I asked, sarcastically.

"No way, not when flippin' Coronation Street is happenin' all round the house. It's great," he replied giddily.

"Yeah I suppose it is to someone who only sees us once a year and can get up and go whenever he likes. I live with these people. It's not so good then," I explained, climbing over his bed to get to mine. He didn't say anything to that.

"So I gather it's all about Sam with an older man?" he asked trying to make conversation.

"Yes, a very older man. I'd rather not talk about it if it's all the same," I replied tucking myself into my own bed and turning away from him.

"Not her fault, she is a free spirit and has a great sense of adventure with it, runs in her genes," he said, gazing up at the ceiling. I turned round and faced him with my head on my pillow.

"Whose genes are those then?" I asked.

"Your father's obviously, he was always getting into trouble when he was Sam's age," he replied. My uncle Jim was my dad's brother and as such was probably the main reason why he was a complete wanker. However I was keen to know more about my dad so I asked, "Has my dad always been the way he is now?"

"Nah, no way, he was just like you up to his forties," he

explained. I was surprised at that.

"Really?" I said, "what changed him then?"

"Well it all went downhill from the moment he split with ya Mam, then his failure to become a big comedian. He needs to get a grip," he said in disgust.

"You not like him much then?" I asked.

"It's not that I don't like him, I don't like what he's become," he replied. It was really strange lying there and listening to my uncle Jim actually make sense and sound as if he was more than an amoeba. I was starting to think I 'd portrayed him a bit unfairly. "I don't like what he has become either. He didn't like it when he found out I'd impressed at comedy club," I said.

"That's just coz' he's frustrated about not making it himself. He angers over anybody else making it, but deep down I know he's proud of ya, kid," said uncle Jim with a smile. I took the last part of his sentence and repeated it over and over in my head. My dad being proud of me was a feeling I could never remember having. The repeated words in my head made me smile broadly. "Thanks, Jim," I said.

"No problem kid, and now you know better, call me your favourite uncle Jim," he said, smiling.

54

6

Pressed Charges

The next morning came with hopes of a normal day. I got out of bed, surprisingly finding that uncle Jim was not there. It was the day before my show so I planned to do some much-needed revising as well as writing some new material down. I sat down at my desk when my mobile phone rang. I picked it up and answered it. I recognised the voice immediately, it was the bird from the bus stop. "Shit, you've got to remember her name soon," I whispered fiercely to myself, my hand covering the phone so she couldn't hear. I chatted to her for a while and told her where my show was going to be and she said she'd come. I had just said goodbye and put the phone down when Steven barged in.

"Aren't you supposed to be at school?" I asked.

"Study leave," he said quickly. "Pigs are at the door for you." I turned around.

"You're jokin'," I replied. I got dressed and went downstairs and sure enough there were two coppers stood at my front door. "Mr. John Massey?" asked one of them.

"Yeah," I replied. "You're not saying my dad's in again?"

"No, we want you today, sir," replied the second officer. I was stunned.

"And why's that, then?" I replied in a voice a little too cocky.

"A Mr. Stanley O'Connor is pressing charges against you for an assault yesterday afternoon," the officer replied.

"Stanley O'Connor?" I said trying to rack my brains. I didn't even know a Stanley O'Connor. Suddenly there was a voice from behind me.

"That man I was kissing yesterday - you know - the one you flattened?" Sam said before turning away sighing. I couldn't believe it - the jammy bastard was pressing charges!

"If you would like to come with us to the station, sir," he said and he led me out of the house.

I got in to the back of the car and the coppers got in the front. One of them turned around and said, "Let's just hope this is the first and last time you see the back of a police car, son."

I rolled my eyes and didn't reply. Bloody pigs. I was taken to the station and sat in the same room as before. I wasn't in there as long as the last time however. They took me in and gave me a quick game of twenty questions. I told them everything that happened and said that the only reason I hit the bloke was because he was snogging my fifteen-year-old sister. The Scouse had obviously been interviewed before me because they knew that he thought she was eighteen, which she had told him. But then I had a thought of my own - what

56

proof did he have that she told him she was eighteen? If I could get Samantha to tell the officers she said she was fifteen and he said he was younger than what he was, we could press charges against him! It was perfect. I had been a comedian, Rambo and now detective Columbo in the space of three days. I told the officers the lie I had just thought of and that we had not pressed charges earlier because we felt it best to leave it in the past. They ate it like I served it on a hot plate. They asked me if I could bring Samantha in to give a statement and have a game of twenty questions also. I agreed so they let me out on bail, for the time being.

I stepped out of the station feeling quite pleased with myself. All the way home I tried to think of ways I could persuade Sam to go along with my plan. I wasn't even completely sure if she was talking to me. When I arrived home I asked Steven where she was and he directed me to her bedroom. I walked up slowly and came to her door, giving it a little tap. There was a brief pause before a lock clicked and the door opened, revealing Samantha.

"What?" she said blankly.

I looked beyond Sam and had a gander at the inside of her room. The floor was trashed with paper and toiletries, as well as her desk. Posters of posers and puffs lined her walls, one wall was totally dedicated to some boy band I had never heard of. "Fancy a ticket to see them next time they're in Manchester?" I asked pointing towards the posters of the boy band. "Like you could afford them," she replied sarcastically. She was obviously right. "Well, I will be able to when I'm a top comedian," I replied.

57

She tried to hide back a smile but it came through, showing her the dimples in her cheeks.

"What do you want?" she asked coolly.

"It's a long story," I replied gesturing inside her room. She sighed and let me in and I told her everything about the charges. She sat for a while and thought about it before giving a cheeky smile. "You know I could just turn round to you and say your bed, you lie in it," she proclaimed.

"Yes, but then I could turn round to you and say buy your own ticket," I replied, batting the ball back in her court.

"You can't afford the ticket. It would take you a while to raise the cash," she said, smashing the ball back fiercely.

"It would take me longer with a big fine to pay on my back," I said. She thought for a moment, showing signs of defeat, so I hit the finishing ball. "C'mon, Sam he's nothing to you now, he's Scouse for God's sake!" I said.

"Ok then," she sighed. Game, set and match, John Massey.

"Nice one, Sam," I said, hugging her. She pushed me away; I had forgotten who I was negotiating with. "When do I need to go to the station?" she asked.

"We don't have to," I said rubbing my hands. "You know where he lives don't ya?" She shook her head and looked away. "Don't lie to me Sam, you must have been to his house." She turned around and looked me in the eye.

"Ok, I've been to his house but don't tell Mam!" she said, poking me.

"I'm not going to tell, if you take me to his house."

"Why you want to go there?" she asked, mystified.

"I want to introduce Stanley to a mate of mine called Bribe," I explained cheekily. I sat up and walked out of the room calling for Sam to follow me. We made our way out of the house and Sam led the way to his house. It was only a few roads past the park they met up at. He lived in a small flat above a cafe. "Nice," I said sarcastically turning to Sam. I knocked on the cafe door and shuffled my feet impatiently waiting for an answer. There was an odd rustling sound from inside until the door was eventually opened with Stanley on the other side. "What do you want!?" he scowled.

"Unless you want the whole town thinking you're a paedophile I suggest we talk inside," I said, pushing him aside without a reply. I walked through the cafe and up a flight of stairs into his flat, with Sam following behind me. Inside the front room were two settees and a television and in the corner stood a blue motorbike. "How the hell have you got that up here?" I asked, baffled.

"Is that what you came here for, to ask about my bike?" he asked leaning against the front room door frame. Samantha did not even look at Stanley; she just sat on one of the settees and said nothing. "No," I replied coolly, "I came to ask you...no...tell you to do something." I strutted around the room, talking as if I was the leader of the mob.

"Oh really, and what's that, like?" he replied sighing.

"Drop the charges," I said looking him in the eye. You would think it was the best joke I had ever told as he roared in fake laughter.

"I don't think I'll be doing that, mate," he said, taking a step closer to me.

"If you don't drop the charges, we'll make one against you," I said staring him in the eye. He raised an eyebrow. "What charges?" he asked.

"Abusing and lying to my sister by telling her you're only eighteen," I said winking at him.

"Ha!" he blurted, "I think you're gettin' mixed up, mate, it's that one that said she's eighteen," he said, gesturing towards Sam. She was trying to ignore us both by looking around the room, taking a strange interest in the motorbike. "Can't prove that to the police can you?" I asked cunningly. He stopped and fell silent for a few seconds; I could see his brain working behind his eyes. "It's not as if I had sex with her," he said.

"Can't prove that either, if you did or didn't. And she's only fifteen," I said shooting a glance towards Sam. She caught my eye and quickly turned away continuing her fake fascinated interest in the bike. I did not know whether what I was saying was right or wrong but I could see that Stanley was no desk sergeant himself. He was threatened by what I was saying and I could see it by the way he was twiddling his fingers and biting his lip. "Think about it," I said, as I sat down turning the TV on, giving him time to boil in the stew.

"Alright I'll drop the charges!" he said, annoyed.

"I knew you would see sense," I said getting up. "C'mon, Sam." She got up and walked out and down the stairs without a word. I followed her out of the front room leaving Stanley behind rubbing his head. I turned to him just before I left and blew him a kiss. "Bye, babes."

I walked back out through the café door and smiled at Samantha who surprisingly smiled back. "Just what did you see in him?" I asked shrugging my shoulders and shaking my head.

"His bike?" she replied, smiling.

"I see," I said.

"You are so chuffed with yourself aren't you?" she asked as we started to walk home. I just smiled and put my hands in my trouser pockets. "What you going to do next, Mr. Massey, get away with murder?" she jibed.

"Nope. I know what I'm going to do now though," I said, stopping in my tracks.

"What?"

"You go home. I'll see you later," I said, as I walked across the road in the opposite direction. Sam shrugged her shoulders and continued to her way home. I was off to see my dad. On my way to his house I saw a man in a brown duffel coat walking out of a baker's. "Y'alright Ken?" I asked as he turned around.

"Oh hi mate, didn't see you there, how ya keeping?" he asked wiping gravy from his pie from his stubbly chin.

"Not too bad," I replied.

"Looking forward to tomorrow night?" he asked, playfully giving me a dig in the arm. The thought of the show had completely left my mind as I had been occupied with other things the past few days. I suddenly realized I had done no revising or writing at all.

"Yeah, can't wait," I gulped.

"Me neither, mate, me neither," he replied. "Listen, I've got some things to sort. I'll see you tomorrow." He pulled out his car keys and pointed them at a fancy Mercedes Benz parked against the pavement. It was one of those keys where you press a button and it opens it from where you're standing, just to prove to the people around you that you're suave and have an expensive car. I waved goodbye as he sped off and continued my journey to the old man's.

I walked up to the door of his flat and gave it a knock, to which he surprisingly answered. "Oh...y'alright, Dad?" I said. He did not say anything, instead he just sighed, turned around and walked back inside leaving the door open. It was my dad's way of saying I could come in without sounding like he liked me. I followed him inside to the usual shit tip that was his front room. He sat down and opened a can of Special Brew, taking a huge gulp from it. I sat down nervously on a chair opposite him, he reached down the side of his settee and pulled another can and threw it in my direction. I caught it before it kissed my face. Due to the awkwardness and surprise of my dad being nice for a change, I opened the can without thinking about it, causing it to fizz all over me. My dad just shook his head and took another swig from his can.

"Cheers, Dad," I said wiping myself down. He said nothing. I took a sip of the beer and sat back. I cringed as the beer was warm, but thought I had to drink it because my dad gave it me. There were two reasons for this; one was because I didn't want to seem like a lightweight in front of my dad and the other was because it meant one less beer for him. I didn't like the thought of what he'd do to me if I wasted it, either.

"How ya keepin'?" he asked, while turning the TV on. I was startled, he was actually asking me how I was.

"I'm alright Dad, you?" I replied. He turned around and raised an eyebrow to me, I laughed.

"Enough said."

"How's Ste and that?" he asked, still facing the television screen.

"Causing trouble," I replied. He half smiled. I knew the fact they were causing trouble for me Mam pleased him. We sat and watched TV, drinking warm beer for about an hour in silence. The six o'clock news came on and my dad switched it off murmuring, "Bloody news, always on about what's goin' on in every country except this one." I smiled.

"You not out tonight, Dad?" I asked trying to make conversation.

"How can I?" he replied and rolled up his trouser leg to reveal an electronic tag. "I'm bloody tied to this place by a pissin' tamagotchi, it's like bein' bloody married all over again," he complained. I let out a loud laugh, dribbling beer down my chin.

"When did ya get that?" I asked still chuckling.

"Pissin' Judge ordered me to have one, on the count of repeat offences."

"That mean you gotta be in for a certain time?"

"Yeah," he replied getting up to stretch. "Still, its better than being in custody." He walked towards what should be

63

known as a kitchen but what could only be described as a reservoir. Mouldy food lined the sides, the floor was soaked and grime decorated the place like a spreading disease. I finished the remainder of my can and placed it on the floor beside the chair.

"I best be off, Dad," I said. He didn't reply as he poked around the cupboards for something. "Seeya, then," I said and walked out of his flat and made my way home.

7

Second Show Time

The next day was pretty boring compared to the previous few, I did nothing but catch up on well-needed revision. I actually went as far as to set a routine and practise it in front of my mirror. I wasn't as worried this time as I was before; I knew I was good enough and that brought confidence. I arrived at Ken's LaughSomeMore comedy club an hour before show time and strutted about like I owned the place. I even went and gave some advice to some young hopefuls who were making their own debuts. I didn't seem to realize this was only my second show and I was still a young hopeful. I met up with Ken before the show and we had a little chat; he told me that he was arranging a tour in a month's time for a selection of the finest new comedians around the country. He did not decide the comedians alone as he had a panel of co-workers who had a say, so he told me to put on an extra special show. Ken seemed to be taking a shine to me; he told me he wanted me on that tour.

I was in my changing room having a drink when a knock came on the door. It was Darren. "Y'alright, funny man?" he asked, popping his head around the door.

"Better than ever, yourself?" I replied smiling.

"I'm like a kid in a sweet shop! Have you seen the talent out there?" he asked excitedly.

"No, not yet, few lookers are there?" I replied. He nodded and rubbed his hands together. Just then I suddenly remembered about asking that bird from the bus stop to come to the show. I ran out of my dressing room towards the stage area and opened the curtain just a little so I could see the audience. She had taken a seat in the middle and was alone this time, sipping on a cocktail. "Darren!" I shouted across to the dressing rooms.

"What you want?" he asked on arrival.

"See out there, middle table, sat on her own, sipping cocktail?" I asked pointing without revealing myself behind the curtain.

"I'd say about an eight or nine," he said, squinting his eyes to see clearer. I was pleased that he said that as that was a pretty good rating from Darren; his standards were higher than health and safety. "I don't want you to rate her, fool, that's my date for the night," I said coolly.

"Well played, my son," he said looking shocked.

"The thing is, I don't know her name," I said blankly. He let out a little laugh.

"Not the best of starts, is it?" he asked shaking his head.

"Well, it's not that I don't know it, I forgot it," I explained.

"Oh and that makes it alright now does it?" he said, still smiling.

"I swear it begins with H…Helen…Heather…something like that."

"Ask her again."

"I did. She thought I was bein' funny," I said quickly. "Could you go out front and get chatting to her, find out her name for us?" I asked, closing the curtain and turning towards him.

"You want me to chat up your date?" he asked, still laughing. I punched him playfully in the arm.

"I'd rather have you smooth her over for five minutes than me make a total arse out of meself asking her name," I explained. He winked at me and turned to walk out to the front.

I toddled back to my dressing room thinking it was best I didn't watch Darren chat up my date; I'd rather not have known what he was saying or doing. I started talking to some of the other lads that were on that night until it was only ten minutes before the show started. I was to be the second act on. I said break a leg to the first act as he walked onto the stage, not knowing what it meant or why people say it. Break a leg, then get charged with GBH and have a criminal record. Maybe that was not the best advice to give him. The empty seat he left behind before going on was shortly filled by Darren.

"You took your time. I said find out her name, not her family medical history," I said sarcastically.

67

"Sorry, I got a bit carried away. She's gorgeous."

"Yes she is, but she still doesn't have a name in my brain," I said impatiently.

"Oh right sorry, her name's Kevin," he joked.

"Stop messin' about what's her name?" I hit him.

"It begins with J, ends in A and has U L I in the middle somewhere."

"Julia, that's it!" I sighed. I sat there and repeated the name over and over inside of my head drumming it into my skull. I could not hear a great deal of laughter from behind the curtain, only the odd titter. It was not long before the first act walked back through the curtains, threw a black top hat he was wearing against the wall and stormed to his dressing room murmuring, "no sense of humour whatsoever."

"I take it he went down a storm," Darren said, lighting a fag.

"I know I will," I said as I got up and prepared myself to go on stage.

A man in an orange suit introduced me on stage as I winked at Darren and walked on. I took a look around the audience as they clapped around their round tables. The audience was noticeably bigger than the last one with a few men with cameras taking pictures below the stage. I spotted Julia in the middle giving out a high pitched whistle, Steven was joined by Darren at the back of the room and uncle Jim had taken another seat at the front. A few tables to the left of him there was a table bigger than the rest where Ken and other men sat with clipboards and pens. I was about to reach out for the microphone when I froze. There was a seat at the very back behind the bar next to the doors and in this seat was my dad. I could not believe it and didn't know what to think. I didn't know whether he was here to see me or do a show of his own. I looked away from him so I didn't distract myself as some of the audience began to cough. I picked up the microphone.

"I'd like to say I'm pleased to be here but I've been here an hour and I'm already sick of the bloody place," I said. The audience gave a little laugh and I knew I had recovered from my little pause.

I was up on stage for about an hour, remembering every part of my practised routine and even adding in new things I thought on the spot. I took the opportunity to make my brother go red as I told a joke about him and pointed him out in the audience. From that moment on he gave me nothing but dirty looks, totally different from the looks Julia was throwing my way. Every now and then I would catch her eyelashes flicking at me as she sipped her cocktail through a straw. The arousing image was destroyed every time she coughed on her drink through laughing, dribbling all over herself. It was probably just as well she did this because a lump in my pants on stage is something I didn't need. During that night's performance, I learnt a lot about myself and how I could perform better. I found that if I focused on inanimate objects, such as tables, at the start of a show, I didn't stutter as much and it was easier to get the crowd going. It was only once the crowd had started laughing I could look at their faces: it was much more encouraging looking at a laughing face rather than an impatient 'hurry up and make me laugh' face. I finished with a sing-a-long, inhaling some helium from balloons tied to the edge of the stage to give myself a Joe Pasquale voice. I walked off stage to tremendous applause, sweat poured down my neck and everyone backstage gave me a pat on the back. Darren came through to the dressing rooms.

"Class, mate, just class," he said wiping a tear from his eye. I smiled. "You'll never guess who's out back," he said hurriedly.

"Dad," I said blankly.

"Yeah, didn't think you'd spot him," he said, raising his eyebrows.

"I'm gonna go have a word with him, you comin' out front?" I asked. He nodded his head and led the way. Once we got out there the third act was on, getting a decent response from the audience. Darren went and sat back with Steven and I walked towards the seat my dad was occupying.

"Y'alright Dad?" I asked and took a seat next to him. He took a swig from his drink.

"I'm alright kid, good show, had the punters in stitches," he said without looking at me.

"Cheers, Dad," I said, beaming with delight at the praise I was receiving from him. It was shocking enough to see him there, never mind have compliments off him. "Not like that choke on before you, couldn't get a laugh if the room was filled with happy gas," he said in disgust. I let out a little laugh. Once you're at the age my dad was you can say things like that in front of anyone; you're not rude - you're a character.

"You staying much longer, doing a show?" I asked. He rolled up his trouser leg to reveal the electronic tag. "Nah, the wife wants me home before nine," he said sighing. I looked at my watch to see the time was almost a quarter to nine. "You best be off then," I said, pointing to my watch.

"Wishing me away, are ya?" he replied getting to his feet. I smiled.

"You seen Steven?" I asked as he finished off his drink.

"Has Steven seen me?" he retaliated.

"Fair play," I replied. "I'll seeya whenever then."

"Alright, kid, seeya." He headed towards the door.

"Nice to see you here," I shouted after him. He raised a hand without turning round and walked out the door.

I watched him go and then went to talk to Darren and Steven. Steven gave me a dig for the joke I told about him and then smiled. He said he had to get back home because The Bill was on and he didn't want to miss it, sad bastard. Darren had scooted off somewhere talent spotting, he had three rubbers in his back pocket and did not plan to finish the night with the same amount. I had a ten pound note in my back pocket and planned to end the night with the same amount. But then I remembered Julia. I had asked her to go out after the show so I looked towards her table. She sat there stirring her drink, looking around, not paying much attention to the third act. I walked up to her.

"Excuse me," I said as she turned around. "I asked the man at the door to lead me to the most gorgeous girl in here and he directed me to this table." She blushed and smiled. A woman, who was sat with three others in front of Julia's table, was looking over at us. She spoke aloud to her friends while still looking our way, "Look at that tart. The main man has only just got off stage an' she's got her claws in him." Julia lowered her head slightly. I could see she was a little intimidated. "She's been givin' him the eye all night, as if she's somethin' special," the woman continued.

"Are you sure the man at the door didn't point you in her direction?" Julia whispered, half smiling.

"What? You mean that blob of a woman who looks like she put Gregg's out of business? The one whose arse is eating her chair?" I asked aloud so she could hear. "No, I'm sure it's you." Julia burst out laughing as the woman turned back around in disgrace, with a face like thunder. The third act had just finished and was walking off to general applause.

"Listen, I have to go backstage a minute to sort out a few things, you be waiting here?" I asked hurriedly. She nodded her head and continued to stir her drink.

8

The Deal and the Date

I walked backstage and met up with Ken and two of the men he was sat with at the table during my show. "There's my man," shouted Ken pointing in my direction. The two men smiled and shook my hand. They took me into a small room with two settees and a table. I sat down and Ken leaned forward in his seat. "How would you like to be doing shows in London, Birmingham and Newcastle?" he asked excitedly.

"Seriously!?" I asked astounded,

"Yeah, the boys and I have decided you're one of the lads we want on this tour."

"How long will it last?" I asked, gob-smacked.

"It's a two week affair, with pay, and we pay for accommodation and such," he explained.

"Well I'd love to but I'd have to talk to my family and stuff."

"Yeah I understand that but listen, these boys are only in town for tonight, then they've got to be off to London," he said, pointing to the two men sat on the opposite settee. One of them leaned forward, opened a briefcase he was carrying and took out some sheets of paper. "These papers are just contracts and legal mumbo jumbo for agreement if you want to join the tour," he explained handing me the papers. I flicked through them picking out odd words and not really reading it. "If you sign this now I can give it these boys and they can be off, but if you change your mind it will only take one phone call and it will be ripped to pieces," he continued to explain. He reached into the inside pocket of his jacket and pulled out a card with his number on it. I looked at the card, then looked at Ken and then looked back at the card trying to think of an answer. "Take your time to make up your mind, kid You can leave it till tomorrow, but it would be handy if you signed this now," he said, rubbing my head and messing my hair the way dads do.

"I'll sign it," I said.

"Excellent," Ken said, rubbing his hands and passing me the papers and a pen. I jotted my name down on three different lines and handed them him back. Ken passed them back to the man and he placed them in his briefcase. I shook Ken's hand and got up to walk out. "You'll have made fifteen by the end of it," he uttered, leading me out.

"Fifteen pounds? I didn't expect to be paid at all, to be honest," I said. Ken stopped and gave a little smile. "Fifteen hundred," he proclaimed, patting me on the shoulder. My eyes widened and my mouth dropped. "A grand an' arf!" I said, shocked.

"Last time comedians were earning fifteen pounds on tour, Tommy Cooper was still around," he said laughing. He said goodbye and I made my way slowly back to Julia's table still trying to take it all in. Fifteen hundred pounds was an amount I had never dreamt of seeing, never mind having in my back pocket. My family was working class and me Mam had a cleaner's job. We weren't exactly wiping our arses with double quilted velvet. The ten pounds in my back pocket wasn't going to be there much longer. I planned to go out and celebrate. I walked up to Julia who was sat with only a few others as all the acts had finished. "C'mon beautiful, get ya coat," I said smiling.

"Yes sir," she said raising her hand to her head and saluting me sarcastically. We walked out through the doors into the cold night air. I looked around the town centre trying to figure out a place we could go. "How old are you, by the way?" I asked inquisitively. I couldn't believe I had not asked that question before, I suppose it didn't really matter. She was old enough to get into the clubs and she certainly wasn't a pensioner; she must have been somewhere in my age range.

"Don't you mean how young am I?" she replied smiling.

"Oh sorry, how young are you?" I asked, cheekily rolling my eyes.

"I'm eighteen, how about you?" I told her my age and whisked her off to some bars and clubs just down the road from where we were.

During the course of the night, I found out she lived with her parents and had recently moved into a house about a twenty minute walk away from me. She was in university doing a course on law and worked at her dad's solicitors in the summer. Hence she wasn't exactly short of money and didn't mind paying for a few rounds; well, most of the rounds. Also, over the course of the night, after I had told her about the tour, she had agreed that she would look over my contracts, making sure they were legit and such. Sorted. We danced, chatted and drank until the early hours of the morning. The time flew by. We laughed so much our ribs ached, until the loony juice numbed the pain. It was about 2am when we decided to call it a night and staggered out of the last club. We were both a little happy as you can imagine and we bundled into a taxi outside the club. I asked the driver if he had been busy as he took us to Julia's home (You have to, don't you?).

"Julia, listen, seriously now…I've got somethin' to say," I slurred, my head spinning. "You know that tour I might be doin' in a month's time? I was wondering if you wanted to come with."

"Aw, I'd love it," she said smiling at me. "But I'll have to ask my dad to give me a few weeks out. I'm sure he will though." The taxi didn't take long before it pulled up outside her house. We got out and I told the driver to stay there. I walked her up her path to her doorstep and she turned around and looked me in the eye. She had to stand on her doorstep before she could do this as she was nearly a foot smaller than me. "I enjoyed tonight," she beamed.

"Me too," I said smiling. She reached into her handbag and gave me a piece of paper with her number on it. "I'd love to go out again sometime," she said smiling sweetly. I took the paper from her hand and put it in my back pocket. I gazed at her as a light attached to her wall outside the door lit up her face beautifully. You know what kind of lights I mean? Those annoying twats who come on when you walk past someone's house, just what exactly is the point in them things? It keeps cats from shagging in your front garden and that's about it.

I gazed at her dreamily.

"Oi! Mister," she barked, still smiling. "My eyes are up here love, not down there." She cupped her breasts in her hands as she said this. I don't know whether it was the effect of the booze but no matter what, she was beautiful. I wanted to kiss her but didn't know how to go about it, I didn't know whether she wanted me to kiss her or not. It was like being a kid all over again. I had never had this problem since leaving school, but there was just something about Julia that made me act weird. I leaned forward a little but the booze made me lose my balance and I fell forward, tripping over her doorstep.

Julia let out a little laugh and caught me before I fell, lifted my head up and said, "Come here ya daft sod." She pulled my head towards hers and planted a sweet kiss on my lips. We stood there for what seemed a lifetime tasting what each other had for dinner until she pulled away. "Goodnight, babes," she said, slowly opening her front door. I so wished at that time she lived on her own. I said goodnight and began to walk back to the taxi when I realized just how long I'd been there kissing.

"Julia," I called urgently, just as she was about to close the door behind her.

"What?" she asked, opening it again.

"You couldn't lend us a few quid for taxi, could ya?" I asked innocently. She laughed and shook her head.

"What are ya like?" she giggled as she pulled out a twenty-pound note from her handbag.

"Nice one! I'll pay you back next time I see you," I said as I took it from her.

"Don't be daft, you'll pay me nothing," she said as she gave me another quick kiss. "Goodnight." She walked back into her home, closing the door behind her. I knew from that moment and from that night that I loved that girl. I loved her handbag also, I wanted one; she had been pulling money from it all night to pay for drinks and things. I walked out of her garden and back to the taxi and told the driver to take me home. The thought of Julia had not left the back of my head since the kiss. I was pent up with excitement from everything that had occurred that night, I was practically bouncing off the doors of the taxi. I felt I had to ring Darren, because you always end up ringing your best mate when you're pissed, just to release some of the excitement by telling him everything. I bragged to him about everything, including the contracts and the tour, but mainly about Julia. The taxi eventually pulled up outside my house, I got out and passed him the twenty pound note and told him to keep the change. In my opinion I think everyone should stop doing that, because now they expect it. Taxi drivers expect a tip so much they even 'tut' when you don't give it them.

I staggered up to my door and opened it quietly. It was around 3am so I was quite surprised to see me Mam sat in the living room watching TV. "Y'alright Mam" I said as I stumbled in. "Why are you up?" I asked.

"Couldn't get to sleep, arthritis playing up again," she replied rubbing her shoulders. She was often riddled with arthritis but 'injured by air' didn't seem to be a good enough excuse for her boss when she tried to get days off work with it. I tried to sit down but had to double check I was sitting on the right one of the three settees I saw swimming before me. "No need to ask where you've been then," she said sighing.

"You should have come to me show, Mam, I went down a storm," I said excitedly. I then went on to tell her about the tour and the contract and everything that Ken proposed to me.

"So are you going to take it?" me Mam asked once I had told her.

"Well I thought I'd talk it over with you first. You don't mind, do ya?" I asked sitting back and slouching.

"You're eighteen now, son. You can look...well, you should be able to look after yourself," she said, scanning me up and down.

"So that's a yes, then?"

"If that's what you want to do," she said smiling.

"Nice one - I'll be earning fifteen hundred quid as well," I said, steadily getting to my feet. Me Mam's mouth dropped. "How much!?" she gasped.

"Fifteen hundred, and keep your voice down, you'll wake up house."

"What you treating me to?" she asked rubbing her hands.

"A new dishwasher," I replied winking as I walked towards the living room door.

"Charming," she muttered.

"I'm going to bed, goodnight Mam," I said, heading for the stairs.

"Goodnight, son," she replied. I took my time walking up the stairs as they kept on moving before my eyes. It was bad enough falling down stairs but I didn't want to look an utter prat falling up them. I eventually made it to the top and staggered across to my bedroom door. I walked in, skipped over uncle Jim and collapsed in my bed. All night I dreamt about Julia.

9

The Start of a Great Relationship

I woke up the next morning at midday and really regretted I had. My stomach churned and the man inside my head must have been knocking down a wall for a kitchen extension. Uncle Jim was sat up watching TV. He said good morning but I ignored him and slumped down the stairs into the kitchen. I fumbled around the medicine cupboard until I eventually found some pain killers.

"Ouch, rough night?" asked Sam as she walked in with her dirty laundry.

"Do I look that bad?" I asked gingerly. She just laughed and walked out again. I sat at the table in the dining room shortly joined by Steven. He patted me on the back and sat down beside me.

"Watch it," I said holding my head.

"Ouch, bet you're glad you didn't stop at that girl's house last night, waking up like you are," he said, taking a newspaper from under his arm and spreading it across the table.

"Who told you about Julia?" I asked puzzled.

"Darren," he replied, "I also heard about this grand and half you're making on some tour." He turned to the sports pages and began to read. "News gets around bloody quick," I said, nursing my forehead.

"Saw you talking to the old man last night, too," he said blankly, without taking his eyes from the paper.

"You don't miss much, do ya," I said. "How come you didn't let on to him?"

"How come he didn't let on to me?" he replied. I sighed and got to my feet, I could not be bothered going into a conversation about Dad with Steven. It was wasted breath.

"I've got to call Ken, anyway," I said and walked back upstairs to my room. As I walked I started to have an idea, which made my head hurt more. I rubbed my head and walked into my room.

"Jim, you don't mind fuckin' off for a few minutes do ya?" I asked as I walked in.

"Why?" he asked with a puzzled, offended look.

"I just got to phone someone and I'd rather do it in private," I explained.

"Not until you ask properly," he asked turning his head. I sighed.

"Please can you fuck off for a few minutes, favourite uncle Jim?" I asked, rolling my eyes.

"Can do," he replied and he got up and left the room,

taking a grungy green dressing gown with him. I had not got undressed before collapsing on my bed the night before so I was still wearing the same clothes. I reached into my back pocket and pulled out two pieces of paper, one with Ken's number on and the other with Julia's. I placed Julia's in my drawer and sat down at my desk and rang Ken.

"Rochdale," he said when he answered.

"Y'alright, Ken, this is John."

"Oh hello, John. You haven't changed your mind, have you?"

"No. I want to do it, but on one condition," I replied.

"What's that, mate?"

"You let me bring my dad and give him a few shows with me on tour."

"You're joking, right?" he choked.

"No, I'm serious." I did not know whether it was a good or bad idea at the time, but I had always wanted to help my dad and I thought I could by doing this. "I don't know if I can do that John. He doesn't fit with the young comedians programme, plus there are difficulties…" he said and then paused.

"It isn't really young comedians though, is it Ken? It's new and upcoming comedians."

"Yeah, but unless you haven't noticed, mate, your old man isn't exactly new or upcoming."

"That aint fair Ken, you must have known him when he first started, he was a class act."

"He's had his chance."

"Let me be his second, we could be a double act," I said pleadingly.

"I don't know…" he said, uncertainly.

"Trust me Ken, I can see it working."

"It seems like your dad has a few more serious issues to solve, don't you think?" he asked sternly. I knew exactly what he meant. It wasn't hard to work out he was a drunk - you only had to look at him.

"I'm working on it," I lied. Actually it wasn't much of a lie. I knew I was going to have to help him solve his alcohol problem anyway. Silence fell as Ken was thinking. "If he doesn't go…I don't go," I said sternly without thinking. I screwed my eyes and hit myself on the head because of what I had just said. I was about to blow my big chance. I could hear Ken breathing and shuffling some papers. "You know you would have to split your pay with him. That means you'll only be getting seven fifty from the tour," he explained.

"Seven fifty will do me," I replied with my fingers crossed.

"And you're sure about this?"

"Yeah, one hundred percent. Please, Ken."

"Ok, Ok, come pick up some papers and have your dad sign them," Ken sighed. I opened my eyes again and breathed a sigh of relief.

"Nice one Ken, you won't regret it," I said and put the phone down. I was so excited I tore off my clothes and got into some fresh ones, pulled on some shoes and ran out the door. I made my way by bus to Ken's office which was above the comedy club. I did not stay there long once I arrived, I just grabbed the papers and set off on the bus to my dad's flat. Once I got off the bus I ran up to his flat and banged on the door with the papers in hand.

"What the bloody hell do you want?" Dad asked, standing at the door in his tacky blue dressing gown.

"Good morning to you too, Dad," I said and I walked into the front room.

"Come in, why don't you? Have a seat," he said, sarcastically, as I slumped on the settee and caught my breath. "What's all this kerfuffle, why you out of breath?" he asked, taking a seat opposite me.

"How would you like to come to London, Birmingham and Newcastle with me?" I asked excitedly.

"What the balls would I want to go down south, or to bloody Brummy or to pissin' Geordie land for?" he blurted with an offended look plastered across his face.

"To do the new comedians tour with me!" I shouted smiling. My dad's eyebrows raised and he looked at me blankly.

"Are you taking the piss?" he asked.

"No I'm deadly serious Dad, I got you on," I said pointing to the papers in my hand.

"I don't know if you have noticed, sunshine, but I don't fall under the category of new or comedian apparently," he said, getting up and storming into the kitchen behind me. He grabbed a can from the fridge and took a huge swig from it.

"I know that, Dad, but I got you in as my double act, plus

85

you'll be getting seven hundred and fifty quid in ya back pocket," I said, turning around to look him in the face.

"That's all well and good. There's just one little tiny problem," he said, moving closer to my face with every word.

"And what's that?" I said quietly as his face was now three inches away from mine.

"To be a comedian, you have to make people laugh," he said spitting in my eye. He took another swig from the can and crashed on the settee turning the TV on. I sat and thought for a while. Although I didn't like to admit it, he was kind of right. I mean I found him funny; he was a real character at times. I remember when I was only young, me mam and dad were still together, we would take trips to Blackpool every year, to see the lights. Every year the old man would buy a wig and one of those fake pair of boobs, put them on and walk around with them on. However, at stand up he was no funny man.

"What if I helped you," I said, turning the TV off and standing in front of it.

"Oh yeah, how you going to do that?" he inquired.

"We've got a month before the tour. What if I helped you with some routines, practised hard and helped you deliver your lines," I said while pacing the room.

"An eighteen-year-old teach me comedy? That's downright insultin'," he said throwing the can into a big pile of rubbish, underneath which must have been a bin.

"Think of it more as putting you on the right tracks, you know comedy…that's your train…you just need a railroad built for you to drive on," I explained, sounding intelligent.

"What's a train got to do with it!?" he shouted.

"Just c'mon Dad, think of what could come from this," I said, placing the papers and a pen in his lap.

"Disaster - it'll never work," he said, pushing them aside. I clenched my fist, I had gone through the trouble of getting this, I was hell-bent on helping him and he was throwing it back in my face. "What have you got to lose, eh!?" I shouted, "You're electronically tagged to a shit hole, you have no job, you're on your own and your only saving grace is the bottom of a bottle!"

My dad sat there with a look of utter shock on his face as I raged down his neck. "Why don't you just see the chance when it's there, Dad, and pick yourself up, man!?"

After all the shouting I sat down and looked him in the eye. He sat there for a few minutes just staring at his feet saying nothing until he picked up the papers and signed on the three lines. He threw them over the room at me and said nothing.

"Right, step one completed. Now we've just got to make you funny," I said rubbing my hands. He still said nothing but just stared at me in bewilderment. "Are you willing to let me help you get you out of this hell hole?" I asked. He looked around him as if he had only just noticed the place.

"Absolutely," he said. I was beginning to think aggression was the way to get through to him.

"And you're willing to do anything that I say to help you get out of here?" I asked standing up again.

"Suppose," he mumbled.

"Great, we can start with your drink problem," I said and I walked around the flat collecting all his cans and bottles in a bin bag. "What the hell are you doing!?" he shouted as I went around the place.

"Trust me - this will help," I said and I threw them outside the front door. My dad just sat there not believing I was doing this, but deep down he knew I was right. "I'll be back to clean this place after I've given these papers to Ken," I said as he sat there watching me scurry about the place.

"What you mean, clean?" he said astounded.

"See ya later, Dad," I said, as I grabbed the papers and walked out the door carrying the bin bag of alcohol with me. I dumped the bin bag in a skip outside of his house and made my way to Ken's comedy club once again. Once I got there I walked into his office and handed him the papers.

"Mr. Rochdale - you have just discovered the best double act since Morecambe and Wise," I said and walked straight back out without a word being said.

10

Teaching an Old Dog New Tricks

Shortly after I had dropped off the papers I picked up some cleaning stuff from my house and headed back to the flat. Surprisingly I worked with my dad who went along with everything I told him in order to clean the place.

"So that's what colour my walls are," he said, gazing at the front room wall we had just scrubbed. I knew if we were to get anywhere with changing my dad's lifestyle we needed to get rid of everything that was bringing him down. We cleared up the kitchen and got some new plates and things to occupy the space left previously in his cupboards by the beer cans. I took down the pine tree from the lampshade and bought a set of plug-in air fresheners. As nighttime fell the place was starting to shine, the bedroom was a bedroom once again and the front room looked homely. I was sure the things I found growing in the bathroom could get my dad arrested for possession of illegal substances. I quickly cleaned the toilet, bath and sink. That night I went home to sleep and left my dad to finish off a few minor jobs in the night. I returned the next day. This was to become a regular schedule over the next month or so. I would arrive at the flat at lunch with two bacon sandwiches, a paper and two cream cakes. We would sit eating while he read the paper and then we would get practising a few routines among ourselves. Then when it would get dark I would return home, go to bed and wait for the morning to start again.

During the course of the month I had taught my dad that he could not be too aggressive during his stand-ups and should not laugh too much at his own jokes. He adapted to my rules pretty quickly and we were soon thinking of material we could use in our double act. My dad would often get frustrated when he messed up a punch line and storm into the kitchen looking for a beer, and then realizing there weren't any would sometimes make him worse. Hence, some days we just sat and watched telly or I went out to see Julia.

I would see her around twice a week and we would go out either clubbing once I had finished with my dad, or we'd go out for something to eat. On our third date, she invited me to come inside her house, which I accepted, obviously. Me Mam would often ask me questions as to where I had been sleeping on the nights I was with Julia so I eventually had to introduce them to one another. Me Mam would often tell us I had a great girl in her, which I already knew but it was nice hearing it from your Mam. We had a few rows during the course of things, mainly about the reason why I never let her stay at my house and was always at hers. I introduced the reason - which was Uncle Jim - to Julia and she soon agreed with me. It was best she did not stay at my house anyway; I could have woken up one morning to find her toothbrush in my bathroom – for keeps.

I knew that my dad was not going to impress on the tour until he had some real practice in front of an audience so we slowly started by inviting Julia round to the flat to watch one of our routines. My dad was really quiet while she was there but seemed to get on with Julia well, occasionally letting out a little of the Massey charm. During the routines she would sit and pretend to laugh and find it funny. I knew she was faking but my dad had not heard a real laugh in his direction in such a long time he didn't know the difference. Although our act was not exactly gold at that time, it wasn't because the act was not funny that she faked a laugh, but doing it in a front room of a flat to one person should not bring expectations of roaring laughter. I respected Julia for trying, though, as I could see the confidence growing in my dad's face like a flower towards sunlight. His confidence was growing, sights set on stardom.

We had to wait a week to do a show with an audience as my dad was still electronically tagged to the flat. Once he had been to the station and had it taken off we booked a show in a small local pub down the road from his flat. I watched my dad sat in the small room behind the bar shaking with nerves. He looked just like me on my first show but he had been playing this game for twenty years.

"Don't worry Dad, it's just a poxy pub," I said, shaking his shoulders. He looked me in the eye and nodded, smiling.

"Son, I can't do it," he said looking at his feet.

"Not with that attitude you can't," I replied.

"No, you don't understand," he said, gesturing towards the bar. It had been almost two weeks since my dad had had a drink. I had completely forgotten all about that. I was so stupid to book a show in a pub; I looked towards my dad whose hands were shaking.

"Fight it Dad," I said placing my hand on his knee. "Once we get on the stage you'll forget all about it," I said softly.

The man behind the bar climbed onto the stage and grabbed a microphone.

"Ladies and Gentlemen. Please welcome your entertainment for the evening…Like Father, Like Son." It's the name we'd gone with - it was my dad's idea. I walked onto the stage with my dad closely following behind me. I picked up one of two microphones on the stage and was about to start the show when my dad interrupted me before I could even breathe down the mike. "Hello, Ladies and Gents. My name's Frank Massey and this…is a result of a knee trembler," he said pointing towards me. All the blokes in the room let out a cheer and the bar man let out a loud laugh. My dad turned towards me and winked, I smiled back at him. I could see it, the magic twinkle in his eye; I knew Frank Massey was back on track.

The night went down a treat; we worked together like butter on toast. I could see my dad slowly building in confidence throughout the show, his head rising a little higher with every minute. The gig we did that night was the easiest I had ever done; I didn't have to worry so much about forgetting my material. With my dad there, I could think of what I was going to say while he was saying his bit. I could tell my dad was learning a lot from the show and me also; when I was speaking I would often catch him looking at me, his eyes concentrating hard – thinking of how he could work off what I was saying. A few times during the show my dad stuttered, but I was there to help him recover, my dad giving me a 'thank you' smile each time. At the end of the show my dad ran into the back punching the air, beaming with joy.

"We did it, we did it. Did you see their faces!?" he shouted, dancing on the spot. I laughed.

"The best is yet to come," I said winking. I calmed my dad down and took him home back to his flat with a kebab in hand. We walked home, joking along the way; I could see the happiness shining through him. I said goodbye once he was home and made my way back to my own. I wished there was someone there I could tell about the night I had just had, but no one would be interested, seeing as it was my dad I'd been with. I went straight to bed and slept until noon the next morning so I was late getting to the flat. I got dressed quickly and skipped the bacon sandwich from the café along the way. I walked up to the flat and noticed that the door was open so I ran towards it and gazed through. My dad was lying on the settee with empty bottles and cans surrounding him. The carpet was stained with sick and the room had been trashed once again.

"You're jokin'!" I screamed as I stampeded into the room. My dad awoke with a start and looked around him trying to gather his thoughts.

"Why, Dad!?" I yelled down his throat. He said nothing and looked at the cans around him. "After all we went through and all we've done!" I continued to rave. My dad lowered his head and a tear rolled down his cheek. I sat down beside him feeling guilty about shouting at him.

"I need help," he said quietly wiping his nose on the sleeve of his jacket. I put my arm around his shoulder, "I know, Dad, and I'm gonna help you through this," I said, squeezing his arm.

From that day I moved into his flat with my uncle Jim's put-up bed and let him sleep in mine for the time being. It gave me time to revise and practise with my dad and help him keep away from the booze. He was very quiet during practices from that day onwards but still got very frustrated, throwing tantrums at times. By the fourth of the four weeks' practice leading up to the tour his need for alcohol seemed to drop a bit. I let him have the odd glass of wine or champagne here and there as I knew taking him completely off the poisons would do no good. The last week before the tour we did a few more shows at local clubs and bars where we went down a real storm, receiving tremendous praise. The local paper had an article about us with pictures of us on stage. By this time my family had clocked on as to what I was doing and me Mam was not too pleased about it but she still gave her support. Steven and Darren came to most of our shows as well as Julia who was also, always, really supportive.

It was the night before we were to go on tour, the next morning we were to meet up at 9am outside Ken's comedy club. I lay in my put-up bed in the front room looking up at the ceiling. "You awake, Dad?" I said loudly into the bedroom opposite.

"Yeah," he replied, shuffling around in his bed.

"Me too."

"No shit, Sherlock! Here's me thinkin' you were sleep talkin'," he said sarcastically.

"You keep that sense of humour up, we'll blow their heads off," I said laughing. He laughed back. I looked towards the clock. It was 2am. I turned to my side and thought back to the days when my dad would throw me out of his flat in disgust. That was the time, when I wished I could be lying where I was. We had come a long way since then, we were like the best of friends and I was so happy about it. Finally, I had a dad. Even if the tour didn't go well and I didn't go on to be a top comedian, I'd be happy that I'd made it this far. I would have to get up at 7 in the morning to make sure we had everything packed and pick up Julia who was coming with us, so I closed my eyes and dreamt of me and Dad on the big stage.

11

The Tour and what Became of It

The next morning was hectic as we rushed around like excited little school girls on a school trip. We made sure we had everything packed, and picked up Julia who was waiting outside her house with three suitcases.

"How long she plannin' on bloody stayin'?" asked Dad jokingly.

The first few shows were set in London, the next in Birmingham and the last in Newcastle. The coach journeys between them all were long but made enjoyable by my dad messing about and causing trouble. All the shows were excellent, set in really posh halls and theatres. There were a total of ten young comedians on the tour and we got on with them really well. My dad would often tell them stories of old comedians he watched as a child. After being with him for a while, I had began to notice that he was often complaining of bad indigestion, so we stopped off at a service station to pick up some Rennies.

The shows in London were excellent. 'Like Father Like Son' was the title we kept and our act was one of the best. My dad would sometimes show off and do a show by himself, then walk backstage and say, "Top that!" He was growing in confidence every show and every show became funnier. My dad and I got tremendous reviews from each place and were offered gigs after the tour had finished. After one of the Birmingham events a bloke in a grey suit told us he was from Channel 4 and wanted us to be in a comedy sketch alongside some of the country's top comedians. That would follow a few months after the tour, but that wasn't the first time we got on the TV.

By the time we had got to Newcastle, storming reviews rewarded us and a television crew recorded the acts for the BBC. Me Mam phoned us at the hotel I was staying at and she was crying after she had seen me on the TV. She told me how proud she and the family were. Samantha rang me to tell me she wanted her ticket to see the boy band I had promised her and Darren rang almost everyday for a chat. Julia was with me every step of the way. She was almost my manageress, dealing with some contracts when I was on the piss with some of the lads from the tour. My dad would tag along sometimes but he was careful on the sauce.

After the tour had finished, 'Like Father Like Son' was becoming well known and many people wanted to sign us but we stuck with Ken and only signed for television appearances and shows. In the space of a year we had travelled the country, starred in a few television programmes and even been on

Richard & Judy. It was amazing how we had only been known for a year but everyone was so startled by our tale of how my dad conquered his alcohol problem and made it as a comedian. We kept the name 'Like Father Like Son' throughout and we even kept the opening line 'I am Frank Massey…and this is a result of a knee trembler' as our trademark. The audience would join in the ending part with my dad.

It was after a show in Bolton, I sat backstage with my dad, wiping my sweaty forehead with a towel. By this time we were doing shows solely and not with other acts. My dad was looking down at his feet fiddling about with a water bottle. "I want to say something to you, son."

"What's that, Dad?" I replied, putting the towel down.

"Thank you," he said placing his hand on mine and looking me in the eye. "Thanks for everything. You've made me a better man." He let go of my hand. I smiled and gave him a playful dig.

"It's alright," I replied.

"Now we can cut the soppy shit and plan the next show," he said, straightening himself up. This was typically my dad; he did not like to show his feelings. I chuckled.

"You've always been a comedian at heart, haven't ya, Dad?" I said smiling.

"No, I haven't," he said, looking back at the ground.

"What you mean, you've always had it in you, just needed bringing out," I explained cheerily.

"No son, a comedian isn't a comedian until someone

laughs…and you made em' laugh son," he said smiling at me. He reached over and gave me a quick hug and a pat on the back then walked off towards the door.

We continued to do shows all over the country with continued support from my family and Julia. My dad received a letter whilst in Liverpool one day from Steven, Sam and Peter. He beamed with delight as he read the words; they had arranged to meet up with him the next time he was back in Manchester. I sent money to me Mam every week as I was earning more than enough, which meant I was the one with the magic purse and not Julia, although one advantage of her being on tour with me was the other magic purse she had, which I could never have but got to dig for gold in.

The last of our tours finished and we headed back home for a few months' rest. Once we got there Julia went home and spent some time with her much-missed family and my dad went about some of his own business. I walked into my house to find me Mam and the family as well as Darren in the living room. They all welcomed me in with cheers and we sat and talked of my travels for ages. After we had caught up on all the gossip, I took a look at me Mam's new dishwasher, handed a much pleased Samantha her ticket and went out on the piss with Darren.

"Where to then, Darren lad?" I asked as we walked out of the house.

"Ken's place," he replied, walking ahead.

"What you mean, Ken's place?" I replied, stunned.

"He's got some news for you, told me to tell you and

then we can go to town," he said hurriedly. He was rushing because he wanted to get into town as soon as possible. Darren was not stupid and he knew that with me having a drink with him, he could pull any bird he liked as I was famous. Once we arrived at Ken's we walked into his little office.

"There's the man! Heard you went down a treat in Cardiff," he said jumping up and shaking my hand.

"Where don't I go down a treat these days?" I asked, smiling cheekily.

"Big head," Darren laughed taking a seat next to the door. "Could we hurry this up? We're wasting valuable 'get Darren a fit bird' time here," he said impatiently.

"Shut up, you," I said playfully and took a seat next to Ken.

"Alright, I'll put it simply as possible…how would you like to do a show in the MEN Arena?" he asked, grinning.

"Seriously?!" I asked, gasping.

"I'm a very serious man, John. You're the joker here, not me."

"I've never done a crowd that big," I said, my eyes wide. It wasn't just the crowd size that took me back, it was the location. The MEN Arena. The centre of my hometown, my home crowd, my life…and I was to do a show there. Never in my wildest dreams had I ever imagined I could be performing on the stage graced by the presence of so many great comedians and acts.

"Well it's not just you, your dad as well," he explained.

"Yeah I know, but still…bloody hell," I said, rubbing

my forehead.

"You're not about to pass this, are you?" he asked surprisingly.

"Am I heck," I replied.

"Great! MEN Arena hosts 'Like Father Like Son' in four months' time," he explained. He gave me some papers to sign and told me all the details, then shook my hand and I left. I could not believe I was doing a show in my home town in such a big place. It was a dream. I rang my dad and told him everything about it (he had a fancy mobile phone by that time) and he sounded as surprised as I was but just as excited. I literally grabbed Darren by the wrist and dragged him to the nearest club, ordering the most expensive bottle to celebrate. I turned to Darren at the bar then gestured around the room at all the girls.

"Take your pick," I said.

12

The Final Curtain

The days and nights leading up to the biggest of shows consisted of nothing but drunken evenings, saucy nights with Julia and writing new material with my dad. The show was going to be televised live but that thought did not seem to bother either one of us anymore; we had been there and done that. It was becoming more and more difficult walking out in the streets without being hassled by people wanting to tell me how funny I was. Each person would walk up to me and say a line or joke from my shows, you know - just in case I forgot.

I used some of my money to buy my family a new house. It was still in Manchester but somewhere a bit nicer with a bit more space. It was only a little further away from Julia's house and we let uncle Jim stay in our old house as he hadn't sorted his relationship out yet. My dad also bought a place of his own somewhere nice. It wasn't the best thing I bought with my money, though: the best of my spending went towards a box at the City stadium. I sat with Darren inside it on big comfy armchairs, sipping champagne. The atmosphere inside was not as good and the fancy food supplied was no substitute for a pie and a pint, so we usually sat in the stands as normal. The fans were great and treated me like a normal City fan coming to see the match which was fantastic.

It was a week before the show and I was going through the last of our practising with my dad. We took our practice sessions a little easy and less seriously then because we knew we didn't really need them. We did an advert for a washing powder and my dad was offered one for Guinness but he turned it down for obvious reasons.

It was the night of the show and we were sat backstage of the MEN Arena twiddling our thumbs, chatting among ourselves. All the family had been given front row seats including Darren, Julia and me Mam's menopause gang who were all suddenly my aunties after I was on the TV. The television crew was setting up their cameras among the audience and the place was starting to fill and buzz with chatter. I turned towards my dad.

"You ready for this?" I said excitedly with my hands shaking.

"Now more than ever," he smiled and shook my knee. He seemed more relaxed than me, which was a bit ironic. I sat down opposite him, twiddling my thumbs nervously, when I noticed him rubbing his left arm.

"What's up with your arm?"

"I dunno. I must of smacked me funny bone against somethin'. My arm's all tingly and sore," he said, grimacing.

"You want anythin' for it?"

"Nah, I'll be alright. You can chuck me one of those Rennies, though," he said pointing to a table behind me.

"Indigestion playin' up again?" I asked, throwing him a tablet. He nodded and rubbed his chest.

"Dunno why though. I've had nothin' to eat since this mornin'," he said, sipping at a glass of water.

"If you get a bit out of sort on stage just let…" I began to say before he interrupted me.

"I'll be fine. Nothing's getting me off that stage, son," he said, smiling and getting to his feet. A man came barging into the dressing room.

"Ten minutes, lads," he said before disappearing again.

"Well then, show time," my dad said, walking towards the door. I got up and followed him towards a set of stairs we would have to walk down to get to the stage. The stairs started right at the top of the arena and led all the way down to the bottom. My dad looked down the stairs at the audience.

"Bloody Nora, you'll have to carry me down there," he said pointing down the stairs.

"Feel free to jump on my back half way down," I said, laughing.

"I'm too old for this," he sighed whilst looking out at the crowd.

"You've only been doing this a year!" I said, laughing and patting him on the back.

"I know," he said smiling, "seems longer though, doesn't it?"

"A lifetime," I replied as a man began to speak across the PA.

"Ladies and Gentlemen, please welcome Like Father Like Son!" he shouted as the audience cheered, whistled and applauded. I turned towards my dad.

"Let's do it," I said and we started to run down the stairs. The crowd roared at the sight of us, clapping frantically. People in the audience shook our hands and patted our backs as we ran down the steep long stairs towards the stage. I looked back as my dad was lagging a bit behind. He was still rubbing his chest and seemed to be short of breath, but he was still smiling and shaking every hand in sight. We passed the VIP seats and Julia gave me a kiss as I reached her, with Darren giving me a wink. We ran onto the stage and picked up our microphones. "Hello I'm Frank Massey…" my dad said, struggling to catch his breath and swaying a little. The audience let out a roar when they joined in. "And that's the result of a knee trembler," they all shouted along with my dad.

We sailed through some of our routines and lapped up all of the cheers and laughter. "That mandatory old couple who think age is a disability…" I said as the audience giggled. My dad took over and began to say, "when you're my age, son, age is a…" until he stopped in his tracks. I was facing the audience at the time so I turned around to see what was wrong. My dad was bending over holding his chest with his faced screwed. I thought it was part of the age gag as the audience continued to laugh. "I suppose you're right, Dad. Old people are a pain in the chest," I said whilst the audience continued to titter. There was no return from my dad as he was still clutching at his chest; he looked to be in serious pain.

"Dad?" I said. Suddenly I realised it was no joke. My stomach did somersaults as I began to panic.

He collapsed onto the stage dropping his microphone beside him. I threw down my microphone and ran towards him. "Dad!" I shouted but I got no reply. The audience had realized that it was not a joke anymore and fell silent as my dad struggled for breath.

People backstage who knew first aid rushed on and tried to resuscitate him there on the stage as the audience were being ushered out of the Arena. All the cameras were turned off and an ambulance was called.

"Dad…c'mon…breathe, please!" I knelt beside him as tears began to well up in my eyes. Steven and Darren came running on stage and dragged me out of the way.

"The ambulance is here, let them do their job, John," they screamed as I went hysterical.

I went with him in the ambulance to the hospital where cameras flashed outside the door as he was rushed in on the bed. They took him into a room where I was not allowed and I had to sit useless in a waiting room. I was shortly joined by Julia and the family. I ran towards Julia and almost crushed her. "I'm sure he'll be alright," she said, trying to comfort me. Steven gave me a hug as the rest of the family sat down silent.

"He just fell….how could…?" I began to stutter, still crying.

"I know mate, we saw it," said Steven quietly.

I sat down and tried to get my head together when the doctor came in with that look on his face, the look you don't want to see. I fell onto Julia's shoulder beside me.

"I'm afraid I have some bad news," the doctor said quietly looking at us all.

"I think we know what you're about to say," said me Mam with tears of her own rolling down her cheeks.

"Frank has had a heart attack...and we tried our best to revive him but we're not going to be able to save him. He has a few moments left," the doctor said slowly and clearly. By this time Julia was crying along with Samantha and Peter who had been quiet throughout the whole thing.

"Why!?" I muttered into Julia's shoulder. "Why now!?"

"If you would like to see him in his last few..." the doctor began to say but stopped.

"I want to see him," I blurted, wiping my eyes.

"Are you sure?" asked me Mam.

"Yes, now," I said, rising to my feet. The doctor led us through a corridor towards a room with double doors.

We walked through to find my dad lying in a bed with a tube in his mouth, machines surrounded him and a sheet covering everything but his shoulders and upwards. A heart monitor beeped softly next to the bed.

"Can I be left alone?" I asked everyone quietly. They all obliged and left the room. I took a seat next to my dad's bed. "Oh Dad," I said crying. I held his hand and looked at him He seemed so peaceful. It reminded me of the first show we did in the pub when he got his first laugh; he looked at one with everything then, as he did there.

"You don't half pick your moments," I said sniffing. "I just want to say, thank you for being my dad, thank you for helping me make it big. Dad. I couldn't have done it with anyone else." I wiped my face dry. "Say hello to Tommy Cooper for me. Take care, Dad, I'll miss you," I whispered, kissing his forehead. I stood up, tears rolling down either cheek, as the line on my dad's heart monitor beside the bed went flat.

My dad passed away to the sound of laughter, which is the way he would have wanted it. It was ironic of him to die on his arse on stage. I said I would have never had done any of it with anyone else and I wasn't about to carry on without him so I gave it all up from that day on.

A comedian isn't a comedian until someone laughs and he and I had just had the final laugh.

The Author

Ian Arnison-Phillips is 15 years old and a pupil at Burnage High School for boys. Ian wrote the opening chapter of A Comedian Isn't a Comedian Until Someone Laughs and was encouraged by his teacher, Helen Carter, to develop it further: this novel is the result.

Writing is in Ian's blood. His grandfather, Jim Arnison, born and raised in Salford, was the *Morning Star's* Northern Correspondent between 1964 – 1990. Jim has written several books including his own autobiography, *Decades*.

A Comedian Isn't a Comedian Until Someone Laughs is Ian's first novel, he is currently working on his second.

"It's rare enough to find a fresh, confident and genuinely funny new writer - but when that writer is only fifteen, it really is something to shout about. Ian Arnison-Phillips' debut novel is an astonishing achievement - assured, highly readable, and as Mancunian as the blood that runs in Ian's veins. I read the first paragraph of 'A Comedian …' in Ian's classroom on a school visit, and begged Helen Carter, his teacher, to let me take it away and read the lot. I couldn't put it down. A huge thanks to Kaye Tew, Alf Louvre and the rest of the team at MMU for letting others have the chance to enjoy Ian's sparky, honest writing."

Sherry Ashworth

"*A Comedian Isn't A Comedian Until Someone Laughs* reflects Ian's honest approach to writing. He writes beautifully about Mancunian life, quite simply, as he sees it and, in the process, takes the reader on an emotional journey that is so touching it is hard to believe it has been written by one so young.

With acute creative vision, Ian presents a series of characters in his novel, including the death-staring Samantha, a personal favourite of mine. However, it is the central portrayal of an intense father / son relationship that truly reflects Ian's writing abilities.

Ian, your passion for writing is beaten only by your passion for City! Congratulations: you've made someone laugh!

Helen Carter (English Teacher, Burnage High School)

112